W9-BDE-842

She Squared Her Shoulders And Told Emilio, "You Don't Scare Me."

He stepped closer. "Are you sure? For a second there, I could swear you looked nervous."

She resisted the urge to take a step back. But not from fear. She just didn't appreciate him violating her personal space. She didn't like the way it made her feel. Out of control. His presence still did something to her after all this time. He would never know how hard it had been to tell him no back then, to wait. So many times she had come this close to giving in. But he had been too much of a gentleman. A genuinely good guy. He had respected her.

Not anymore.

"I know you," she said. "You're harmless."

He moved even closer, so she had to crane her neck to look into his eyes. "Maybe I've changed."

Dear Reader,

I love all of my characters, and all of the stories I write. But every so often I start a story that from day one just feels…*special*. This is one of those stories.

In the first Black Gold Billionaires book, Emilio was a bit of a mystery. Quiet, thoughtful and a little intense—he left an impression on me. It wasn't until I started to write his story that the complexity of his character became clear. On the outside he's confident and successful and take-your-breath-away sexy, but on the inside…well, suffice it to say, there's more to this man than meets the eye.

Then there's Isabelle. At first she seemed so broken down and vulnerable, I was afraid readers would want to give her a firm shake and shout, "Honey, grow a spine for God's sake!" But she had a few surprises for me, as well. By the end of the book I found myself envying her. Wanting to *be* her.

As much as I would love to take all the credit for creating these two, they honestly wrote themselves. And helping them to put their story into words was an exciting, humbling and heartwarming experience. I hope you enjoy them as much as I did.

Until next month…

Michelle

MICHELLE CELMER

ONE MONTH WITH THE MAGNATE

Harlequin Desire

If you purchased this book without a cover you should be aware that this book is stolen property. It was reported as "unsold and destroyed" to the publisher, and neither the author nor the publisher has received any payment for this "stripped book."

Recycling programs
for this product may
not exist in your area.

ISBN-13: 978-0-373-73112-1

ONE MONTH WITH THE MAGNATE

Copyright © 2011 by Michelle Celmer

All rights reserved. Except for use in any review, the reproduction or utilization of this work in whole or in part in any form by any electronic, mechanical or other means, now known or hereafter invented, including xerography, photocopying and recording, or in any information storage or retrieval system, is forbidden without the written permission of the publisher, Harlequin Enterprises Limited, 225 Duncan Mill Road, Don Mills, Ontario M3B 3K9, Canada.

This is a work of fiction. Names, characters, places and incidents are either the product of the author's imagination or are used fictitiously, and any resemblance to actual persons, living or dead, business establishments, events or locales is entirely coincidental.

This edition published by arrangement with Harlequin Books S.A.

For questions and comments about the quality of this book please contact us at Customer_eCare@Harlequin.ca.

® and TM are trademarks of Harlequin Books S.A., used under license. Trademarks indicated with ® are registered in the United States Patent and Trademark Office, the Canadian Trade Marks Office and in other countries.

www.Harlequin.com

Printed in U.S.A.

MICHELLE CELMER

Bestselling author Michelle Celmer lives in southeastern Michigan with her husband, their three children, two dogs and two cats. When she's not writing or busy being a mom, you can find her in the garden or curled up with a romance novel. And if you twist her arm really hard, you can usually persuade her into a day of power shopping.

Michelle loves to hear from readers. Visit her website, www.michellecelmer.com, or write her at P.O. Box 300, Clawson, MI 48017.

To my editor Charles, who has been, and continues to be, an amazing source of support and encouragement. It has been a privilege, a joy and a lot of fun working with you.

One

This was, without a doubt, the lowest Isabelle Winthrop-Betts had ever sunk.

Not even the sting of her father's open palm across her cheek had caused the humiliation she was feeling now thanks to Emilio Suarez, a man she once loved with all her heart and had planned to marry.

Her father had made sure that never happened. And Isabelle couldn't blame Emilio for the bitterness in his eyes as he sat behind his desk in his corner office at Western Oil headquarters, like a king on a throne addressing a local peasant.

Thanks to her husband, Leonard, that was really all she was now. She had gone from being one of the richest women in Texas, to a pauper. Homeless, penniless, widowed and about to be thrown in prison for fraud. And all because she had been too naive and trusting. Because when her husband had put documents in front of her, instead of reading them, she had blindly signed. How could she question the man who had rescued her from hell? Who had probably saved her life?

And the son of a bitch had up and died before he could exonerate her.

Thanks, Lenny.

"You have a lot of nerve asking me for help," Emilio said in the deep, caramel-smooth voice that strummed every one of her frayed nerve endings, but the animosity in his tone curdled her blood. Not that he wasn't justified in his anger, not after the way she'd broken his heart, but she'd had no choice. She didn't expect him to understand that, she just hoped he would take pity on her.

His charcoal gray eyes bore through her, and she fought not to wither under their scrutiny. "Why come to me? Why not go to your rich friends?"

Because his brother, Alejandro, was prosecuting her case. Besides, she had no friends. Not anymore. They had all invested with Lenny. Some had lost millions.

"You're the only one who can help me," she said.

"Why would I want to? Maybe I want to see you rot in prison."

She swallowed the hurt his words caused, that he hated her that much.

Well, he would be happy to learn that according to her lawyer, Clifton Stone, nothing would prevent that now. The evidence against her was overwhelming and her best bet was a plea bargain. And while the idea of spending even another minute in jail terrified her, she was prepared to take full responsibility for her actions and accept any punishment they considered appropriate. Unfortunately, Lenny had gotten her mother involved in his scams, too. After suffering years of physical and emotional abuse from her husband, Adriana Winthrop deserved some happiness. Not to spend the rest of her life in prison. Not for something that was Isabelle's fault.

"I don't care what happens to me," Isabelle told him. "I want my mother's name cleared. She had no part in any of Leonard's scams."

"Leonard's and *your* scams," he corrected.

She swallowed hard and nodded.

One dark brow rose. "So, you're admitting your guilt?"

If blind trust was a crime, she was definitely guilty. "It's my fault that I'm in this mess."

"This is not a good time for me."

She'd seen coverage on the news about the accident at the refinery. The explosion and the injured men. She'd tried to visit him last week, but the front of the Western Oil headquarters building had been crawling with media. She would have waited another week or two, but she was running out of time. It had to be now. "I know it's a bad time and I'm sorry. This couldn't wait."

Arms folded across his chest, he sat back in his chair and studied her. In a suit, with his closely cropped hair combed back, he barely resembled the boy she'd known from her adolescence. The one she had fallen head over heels in love with the instant she'd laid eyes on him, when she was twelve and he was fifteen. Although, it had taken him until college to notice her.

His mother had been their housekeeper and in her father's eyes, Emilio would never be good enough for his precious daughter. That hadn't stopped her from seeing Emilio in secret, fully aware of the price she would pay if they were caught. But they had been lucky—until her father learned of their plans to elope.

Not only had he punished her severely, he'd fired Emilio's mother. He accused her of stealing from them, knowing that no one else would hire her.

She wished her father could see them now. Emilio sitting there like the master of the universe and her begging for his help. He would be rolling in his grave.

See Daddy, he was good enough for me after all. Probably even better than I deserved.

Emilio never would have hurt her, never would have sacrificed her reputation out of greed. He was honest and trustworthy and loyal.

And right now, seriously pissed at her.

"So you're doing this for your mother?" he asked.

Isabelle nodded. "My lawyer said that with all the media attention, it's unlikely that your brother will be willing to deal. She'll serve some time."

"Maybe I'd like to see her rot in prison, too," he said.

She felt her hackles rise. Adriana Winthrop had never been anything but kind to him and his mother. She had done *nothing* to hurt them. She'd only been guilty of being married to an overbearing, abusive bastard. And even that wasn't entirely her fault. She had tried to leave and he'd made her live to regret it.

"Your appearance," he said. "Is it supposed to make me feel sorry for you?"

She resisted the urge to look down at the outdated blouse and ill-fitting slacks she had rummaged from the bag of clothes her mother had been donating to charity. Obviously he'd expected her to be wearing an outfit more suited to her previous station, but when her possessions had been seized, she kept nothing. For now, this was the best she could do.

"I don't feel sorry for you, Isabelle. It seems to me you're getting exactly what you deserve."

That was one thing they could agree on.

She could see that coming here had been a waste of time. He wasn't going to help her. He was too bitter.

Oh, well. It had been worth a try.

She rose from the chair, limp with defeat. Her voice trembled as she said, "Well, thank you for seeing me, Mr. Suarez."

"Sit down," he snapped.

"For what? You obviously have no intention of helping me."

"I never said I wouldn't help you."

Something in his eyes softened the slightest bit and hope welled up inside of her. She lowered herself into the chair.

"I'll talk to my brother on your mother's behalf, but I expect something in return."

She had expected as much, but the calculating look he wore sent a cold chill down her spine. "What?"

"You will agree to be my live-in housekeeper for thirty days. You'll cook for me, clean my house, do my laundry. Whatever I ask. At the end of the thirty days, if I'm satisfied with your performance, I'll talk to my brother."

In other words, he would make her work for him the way his mother had worked for her. Clever. Obviously he saw her plea for help as an opportunity to get revenge. What had happened to the sweet and kindhearted boy she used to know? The one who never would have been capable of dreaming up such a devious plan, much less have the gall to implement it. He had changed more than she could ever have guessed, and it stung to know that it was probably her fault. Had she hurt him so much when she left that he'd hardened his heart?

And what of his *offer?* The day her father died she had vowed never to let a man control her again. But this wasn't about her. She was doing this for her mother. She *owed* her. Besides, she had swallowed her pride so many times since the indictment, she was getting used to the bitter taste.

Despite what Emilio believed, she was no longer the

shy, timid girl of her youth. She was strong now. Anything he could dish out, she could take.

"How do I know I can trust you?" she asked. "How do I know that after the thirty days you won't change your mind?"

He leaned forward, eyes flaming with indignation as they locked on hers. "Because I have never been anything but honest with you, Isabelle."

Unlike her, his tone implied. He was right. Even though she'd had a valid reason for breaking her word, but that hardly seemed worth mentioning. Even if she told him the truth she doubted he would believe her. Or care.

He leaned back in his chair. "Take some time to think about it if you'd like."

She didn't need time. She didn't have any to spare. Less than six weeks from now she and her lawyer would meet with the prosecutor, and her lawyer warned her that it didn't look good. For her or her mother.

This wasn't going to be a pleasant thirty days, but at least she knew Emilio wouldn't physically harm her. He may have become cold and callous, but he had never been a violent man. He'd never made her feel anything but safe.

What if he changed? a little voice in her head taunted, but she ignored it. The decision had already been made.

She sat straight, squared her shoulders and told him, "I'll do it."

Isabelle Winthrop was a viper.

A lying, cheating, narcissistic viper.

Yet Emilio couldn't deny that despite the fifteen years that had passed, she was still the most physically beautiful woman he had ever laid eyes on.

But her soul was as black as tar.

She'd had him duped, all those years ago. He thought

she loved him. He had believed, despite the fact that she was a Winthrop and he was the son of a domestic servant, they would be married and live happily ever after. She told him she didn't care about the money or the status. She would be happy so long as they had each other. And he had fallen for it, right up until the minute he read the article in the paper announcing her marriage to finance guru Leonard Betts. A multi*billionaire.*

So much for her not caring about money and status. What other reason would she have to marry a man twenty-five years older?

When all was said and done, his relationship with Isabelle hadn't been a total loss. She had taught Emilio that women were not to be trusted, and he'd learned from her deceit never to put his heart on the line again.

That didn't mean he wasn't ready to dish out a little good old-fashioned revenge.

As for her being a criminal like her husband, he wasn't sure what to believe. According to the law, if she signed it, she was legally responsible. Now that Leonard was dead, someone had to pay.

Guilty or not, as far as Emilio was concerned, she was getting exactly what she deserved. But he was not prepared to be dragged down with her.

"There's just one condition," he told her.

She nervously tucked her pale blond hair behind her ears. Hair that he used to love running his fingers through. It was once shiny and soft and full of body, but now it looked dull and lifeless. "What condition?"

"No one can know about this." If it got out that he was helping her, it could complicate his chances for the CEO position at Western Oil. He was in competition with COO Jordan Everett and his brother, Nathan Everett, Chief Brand Officer. Both were friends and worthy opponents.

But Emilio deserved the position more. He'd earned it through more hard work than either of them could ever imagine with their Harvard educations that Daddy footed the bill for.

Maybe he was a fool to risk everything he'd worked so hard for, but Isabelle was offering an opportunity for revenge that he just couldn't pass up. After his father died, his mother worked her fingers to the bone trying to provide for Emilio and his three brothers. It was years after being fired by the Winthrops when she finally admitted to her children the verbal abuse she'd endured from Isabelle's father. Not to mention occasional improper sexual advances. But the pay was good, so she'd had no choice but to tolerate it. And after he had fired her, accused her of stealing from them, no respectable family would even think of hiring her.

Now Emilio's mother, his entire family, would finally be vindicated.

"Are you sure you don't want to brag to all of your friends?" Isabelle asked him.

"I'm the chief financial officer of this company. It wouldn't bode well for me or Western Oil if people knew I was in business with a woman indicted for financial fraud. If you tell a soul, not only is the deal off, but I will see that you *and* your mother rot in prison for a very long time."

"I can't just disappear for thirty days. My mother will want to know where I am."

"Then tell her you're staying with a friend until you get back on your feet."

"What about the authorities? I'm out on bond. They need to know where I'm staying. I could go back to jail."

"I'll take care of it," he said. He was sure he could work something out with his brother.

She looked wary, like she thought maybe it was a trick, but clearly she had no choice. She needn't have worried though. Unlike her, he honored his word.

"I won't tell anyone," she said.

"Fine." He slid a pad of paper and a pen across the desk to her. "Write down where you're currently staying and I'll have my driver come by to get you tonight."

She leaned forward to jot down the address. He assumed she would be staying with her mother, or in a high-class hotel, but what she wrote down was the name and address for a motel in one of the seedier parts of town. She really must have been in dire straits financially. Or she was pretending to be.

Several million dollars of the money they had stolen had never been recovered. For all he knew, she had it stashed somewhere. Of course, if she had been planning to run, wouldn't she have done it by now? Or was she waiting to cut a deal for her mother, then intending to skip town?

It was something to keep in mind.

"Be ready at seven," he told her. "Your thirty days will start tomorrow. Agreed?"

She nodded, chin held high. She wouldn't look so proud when he put her to work. Isabelle had never lifted a finger to do a thing for herself. He was sorry he wouldn't be home to witness what he was sure would be a domestic disaster.

The thought almost made him smile.

"Do you need a ride back to the hotel?" he asked.

She shook her head. "I borrowed my mother's car."

"That must be a change for you. Having to drive yourself places. It's a wonder you even remember how."

He could tell that she wanted to shoot back a snarky comment, but she kept her mouth shut and her eyes all but dared him to give it his best shot. She was tough, but she had no idea who she was dealing with. He wasn't the naive, trusting man he'd been before.

He stood and she did the same. He reached out to shake on the deal, and she slipped her finely boned hand into his—her breath caught when he enclosed it firmly, *possessively*. Though she tried to hide it, being close to him still did something to her. Which was exactly what he was counting on. Because bringing her into his home as a housekeeper was only a ruse to execute his true plan.

When they were together, Isabelle had insisted they wait until they were married to make love, so he had honored her wishes for a torturous year. Then she left him high and dry. Now it was time for some payback.

He would seduce Isabelle, make her want him, make her *beg* for it, then reject her.

By the time he was through with her, prison would seem like Club Med.

Two

"Is that who I think it was?"

Emilio looked up from his computer to find Adam Blair, the current CEO of Western Oil, standing in his office doorway. He should have known word of his *visitor* would get around fast. Her disguise—if that had been her intention with the ridiculous clothes, the straight, lifeless hair and absence of makeup—not to mention the fake name she had given the guards when she insisted on seeing him, obviously hadn't worked. When he saw her standing there in the lobby, her shoulders squared, head held high, looking too proud for her own good, he should have sent her away, but curiosity had gotten the best of him.

Emilio had warned Adam months ago, just before news of the Ponzi scheme became public, that he had a past connection to Isabelle. But he'd never expected her to turn up at his office. And he sure as hell hadn't considered that she would have the audacity to ask for his help. She was probably accustomed to getting exactly what she wanted.

"That was Isabelle Winthrop-Betts," he told Adam.

"What did she want?"

"My help. She wants her mother's name cleared, and she wants me to talk to my brother on her behalf."

"What about her own name?"

"She more or less admitted her guilt to me. She intends to take full responsibility for everything."

Adam's brows rose. "That's…surprising."

Emilio thought so, too. With a federal prosecutor for a sibling, he had heard of every scheme imaginable from every type of criminal. Freely admitting guilt wasn't usually one of them. Isabelle was clearly up to something. He just hadn't figured out what. He had considered that she and her mother were planning to take the unrecovered money and disappear, but why bother exonerating her first? Maybe he could gain her trust, encourage her to tell him her plans, then report her to the authorities.

"So, will you help her?" Adam asked.

"I told her I would talk to Alejandro." Which he still had to do, and he wasn't looking forward to it.

"Also surprising. The last time we talked about her, you seemed awfully bitter."

Not only was Adam a colleague, he was one of Emilio's closest friends. Still, he doubted Adam would even begin to understand his lust for revenge. He wasn't that kind of man. He'd never been betrayed the way Emilio had. Emilio would keep that part of his plan to himself. Besides, Adam would no doubt be opposed to anything that might bring more negative press to Western Oil.

What he didn't know wouldn't hurt him.

"Call me sentimental," Emilio said.

Adam laughed. "Sorry, but that's the last thing I would

ever call you. Sentimental isn't a word in your vocabulary, not unless it's regarding your mother. Just tell me you're not planning on doing something stupid."

There were many levels of stupid. Emilio was barely scratching the surface.

"You have nothing to be concerned about," he assured Adam. "You have my word."

"Good enough for me." Adam's cell buzzed, alerting him that he had a text. As he read it, he smiled. "Katy just got to the house. She's staying in El Paso for a few days, then we're driving back to Peckins together."

Katy was Adam's fiancée. She was also his former sister-in-law and five months pregnant with their first child. Or possibly Katy's dead sister's baby. They weren't sure.

"Have you two set a date yet?" Emilio asked.

"We're leaning toward a small ceremony at her parents' ranch between Christmas and New Year's. I'll let you know as soon as we decide. I'd just like to make it official before the baby is born." Adam looked at his watch. "Well, I have a few things to finish before I leave for the day."

"Send Katy my best."

Adam turned to leave, then paused and turned back. "You're sure you know what you're doing?"

Emilio didn't have to ask what he meant. Adam obviously suspected that there was more to the situation than Emilio was letting on. "I'm sure."

When he was gone, Emilio picked up the phone and dialed his brother's office.

"Hey, big brother," Alejandro answered when his secretary connected them. "Long time no see. The kids miss their favorite uncle."

Emilio hadn't seen his nephews, who were nine, six and two, nearly often enough lately. They were probably the closest thing he would ever have to kids of his own, so he tried to visit on a regular basis. "I know, I'm sorry. Things have been a little crazy here since the refinery accident."

"Any promising developments?"

"At this point, no. It's looking like it may have been sabotage. We're launching an internal investigation. But keep that between us."

"Of course. It's ironic that you called today because I was planning to call you. Alana had a doctor's appointment this morning. She's pregnant again."

Emilio laughed. "Congratulations! I thought you decided to stop at three."

"We did, but she really wanted to try for a girl. I keep telling her that with four boys in my family, we'd have better luck adopting, but she wanted to give it one more try."

Emilio couldn't imagine having one child now much less four. There had been a time when he wanted a family. He and Isabelle had talked about having at least two children. But that was a long time ago. "Are the boys excited?" he asked his brother.

"We haven't told them yet, but I think they'll be thrilled. Alex and Reggie anyway. Chris is a little young to grasp the concept."

"I don't suppose you've heard from Estefan," Emilio asked, referring to their younger brother. Due to drugs, gambling and various other addictions, they usually only heard from him when he needed money or a temporary place to crash. Their mother lived in fear that one day the phone would ring and it would be the coroner's office asking her to come down and identify his body.

"Not a word. I'm not sure if I should feel worried or relieved. I did get an email from Enrique, though. He's in Budapest."

Enrique was the youngest brother and the family nomad. He'd left for a summer backpacking trip through Europe after graduating from college. That was almost three years ago and he hadn't come home yet. Every now and then they would get a postcard or an email, or he would upload photos on the internet of his latest adventures. Occasionally he would pick up the phone and call. He kept promising he'd be home soon, but there was always some new place he wanted to visit. A new cause to devote his life to.

Emilio and Alejandro talked for several minutes about family and work, until Emilio knew he had to quit stalling and get to the point of his call. "I need a favor."

"Anything," Alejandro said.

"Isabelle Winthrop will be checking out of her motel this evening. As far as your office is concerned, she's still staying there."

There was a pause, then Alejandro muttered a curse. "What's going on, Emilio?"

"Not what you think." He told his brother about Isabelle's visit and his "agreement" with her. Leaving out his plan to seduce her, of course. Family man that Alejandro was, he would never understand. He'd never had his heart broken the way Emilio had. Alana had been his high school sweetheart. His first love. Other than a short break they had taken in college to explore other options—which lasted all of two weeks before they could no longer stand to be apart—they had been inseparable.

"Are you completely out of your mind?" Alejandro asked.

"I know what I'm doing."

"If Mama finds out what you're up to, she's going to kill you, then she's going to kill *me* for helping you!"

"I'm doing this for Mama, for *all* of us. For what Isabelle's father did to our family."

"And it has nothing to do with the fact that Isabelle broke your heart?"

A nerve in his jaw ticked. "You said yourself that she's guilty."

"On paper, yes."

"She all but admitted her guilt to me."

"Well, there've been developments in the case."

Emilio frowned. "What kind of developments?"

"You know I can't tell you that. I shouldn't be talking to you about this, period. And I sure as hell shouldn't be helping you. If someone in my office finds out what you're doing—"

"No one will find out."

"My point is, it won't just be your job on the line."

He hadn't wanted to pull out the big guns, but Alejandro was leaving him no choice. "If it weren't for me, little brother, you wouldn't be in that cushy position."

Though Alejandro had planned to wait until his career was established for marriage and kids, Alana had become pregnant with Alex during Alejandro's last year of law school. With a wife and baby to support, he couldn't afford to stay at the top-notch school he'd been attending without Emilio's financial help.

Emilio had never held that over him. Until now.

Alejandro cursed again and Emilio knew he had him. "I hope you know what you're doing."

"I do."

"I'll be honest though, and you did not hear this from me, but with a little more pressure from her lawyer, we would have agreed to a deal on her mother's charge. She would have likely come out of this with probation."

"Isabelle's lawyer told her you wouldn't deal."

"It's called playing hardball, big brother. And maybe her lawyer isn't giving her the best advice."

"What do you mean?"

"I'm not at liberty to say."

"Is he a hack or something?"

"Not at all. He was Betts's lawyer. Clifton Stone. A real shark. And he's representing her *pro bono*."

"Why?"

"She's broke. All assets were frozen when she and Betts were arrested, and everything they owned was auctioned off for restitution."

"Everything?"

"Yeah. It was weird that she didn't fight for anything. No clothes or jewelry. She just gave it all up."

"I thought there was several million unrecovered."

"If she's got money stashed somewhere, she's not touching it."

That could have simply meant that the minute her mother's name was cleared, she would disappear. Why pay for a top-notch defense when she wouldn't be sticking around to hear the verdict? The crappy motel and the outdated clothes could have all been another part of the ruse.

"So why is her lawyer giving her bad advice?"

"That's a good question."

One he obviously had no intention of answering. Not that it mattered to Emilio either way.

"Are you sure this is about revenge?" Alejandro asked.

"What else would it be?"

"All these years there hasn't been anyone special in your life. What if deep down you still have feelings for her? Maybe you still love her."

"Impossible." His heart had been broken beyond repair, and had since hardened into an empty shell. He had no love left to give.

* * *

Emilio had a beautiful house. But Isabelle wouldn't have expected any less. The sprawling stucco estate was located in one of El Paso's most prestigious communities. She knew this for a fact because, until she married Lenny, she used to live in the very same area. Her parents' home had been less than two blocks away. Though she was willing to bet from the facade that this was even larger and more lavish. It was exactly the sort of place Emilio used to talk about owning someday. He'd always set his sights high, and it looked as though he'd gotten everything he ever wanted.

She was happy for him, because he deserved it. Deep down she wished she could have been part of his life, wished she still could be, but it was too late now. Clearly the damage she had done was irreparable. Some people weren't meant to have it all, and a long time ago she had come to terms with the fact that she was one of those people.

Not that she was feeling sorry for herself. In fact, she considered herself very lucky. The fifteen years she had been married to Lenny, she'd had a pretty good life. She had never wanted for a thing. Except a man who loved and desired her, but Lenny had loved her in his own way. If nothing else, she had been safe.

Until the indictment, anyway.

But she would have years in prison to contemplate her mistakes and think about what might have been. All that mattered now was clearing her mother's name.

The limo stopped out front and the driver opened the door for her. The temperature had dipped into the low fifties with the setting sun and she shivered under her light sweater. She was going to have to think about getting herself some warmer clothes and a winter jacket.

It was dark out, but the house and grounds were well lit. Still, she felt uneasy as the driver pulled her bag from the back. He set it on the Spanish tile drive, then with a tip of his hat he climbed back into the limo. As he drove off, Isabelle took a deep breath, grabbed her bag and walked to the porch, a two-story high structure bracketed by a pair of massive white columns and showcased with etched glass double doors. Above the door was an enormous, round leaded window that she imagined let in amazing morning light.

Since Emilio knew what time she was arriving, she'd half expected him to be waiting there to greet her, but there was no sign of him so she walked up the steps and rang the bell. A minute passed, then another, but no one came to the door. She wondered if maybe the bell was broken, and knocked instead. Several more minutes passed, and she began to think he might not be home. Was he held up at the office? And what was she supposed to do? Sit there and wait?

She had a sudden sinking feeling. What if this was some sort of trick? Some sick revenge. What if he'd never planned to let her in? Hell, maybe this wasn't even his house.

No, he wouldn't do that. He may have been angry with her, he may have even hated her, but he could never be that cruel. When they were together he had been the kindest, gentlest man she had ever known.

She reached up to ring the bell one last time when behind her someone said, "I'm not home."

Her heart slammed against her rib cage and she spun around to find Emilio looking up at her from the driveway. He wore a nylon jacket and jogging pants, his forehead was dotted with perspiration and he was out of breath.

Still a jogger. Back in college, he'd been diligent about

keeping in shape. He'd even convinced her to go to the gym with him a few times, but to the annoyance of her friends, her naturally slim build never necessitated regular exercise.

He stepped up to the porch and stopped so close to her that she could practically feel the heat radiating off his body. He smelled of a tantalizing combination of aftershave, evening air and red-blooded man. She was torn between the desire to lean close and breathe him in, or run like hell. Instead she stood her ground, met his penetrating gaze. He'd always been tall, but now he seemed to tower over her with the same long, lean build as in his youth. The years had been good to him.

He looked at her luggage, then her. "Where's the rest?"

"This is all I brought."

One dark brow rose. A move so familiar, she felt a jab of nostalgia, a longing for the way things used to be. One he clearly did not share.

"You travel light," he said.

Pretty much everything she owned was in that one piece of luggage. A few of her mother's fashion rejects and the rest she'd purchased at the thrift store. When the feds had seized their home, she hadn't tried or even wanted to keep any of the possessions. She couldn't stand the thought of wearing clothes that she knew had been purchased with stolen money.

The clothes, the state of the art electronic equipment, the fine jewelry and priceless art had all been auctioned off, and other than her coffee/espresso machine, she didn't miss any of it.

Leaving the bag right where it was—she hadn't really expected him to carry it for her—Emilio turned and punched in a code on the pad beside the door. She heard a click as the lock disengaged, and as he opened the door the lights automatically switched on.

She picked up her bag and followed him inside, nearly gasping at the magnificence of the interior. The two-story foyer opened up into a grand front room with a curved, dual marble stairway. In the center hung an ornately fashioned wrought iron chandelier that matched the banister. The walls were painted a tasteful cream color, with boldly colored accents.

"It's lovely," she said.

"I'll show you to your quarters, then give you a tour. My housekeeper left a list of your daily duties and sample menus for you to follow."

"You didn't fire her, I hope."

He shot her a stern look. "Of course not. I gave her a month paid vacation."

That was generous of him. He could obviously afford it. She was thankful the woman had left instructions. What Isabelle knew about cooking and cleaning could be listed on an index card with lines to spare, but she was determined to learn. How hard could it be?

Emilio led her through an enormous kitchen with polished mahogany cabinets, marble countertops and top-of-the-line steel appliances, past a small bathroom and laundry room to the maid's quarters in the back.

So, this was where she would spend the next thirty days. It was barely large enough to hold a single bed, a small wood desk and padded folding chair, and a tall, narrow chest of drawers. The walls were white and completely bare but for the small crucifix hanging above the bed. It wasn't luxurious by any stretch of the imagination, but it was clean and safe, which was more than she could say for her motel. Checking out of that hellhole, knowing she would no longer wake in the middle of the night to the sound of roaches and rodents scratching in the walls, and God only knows what sort of illegal activity just outside her door, had in itself almost been worth a month of humiliation.

She set her bag on the faded blue bedspread. "Where is your housekeeper staying while I'm here?" she asked. She hoped not in the house. The idea of someone watching over her shoulder made her uneasy. This would be humiliating enough without an audience.

"She's not a live-in. I prefer my privacy."

"Yet, you're letting *me* stay," she said.

Up went the brow again. "I could move you into the pool house if you'd prefer. Although you may find the lack of heat less than hospitable."

She was going to have to curb the snippy comments. At this point it probably wouldn't take much for him to back out of their deal.

He nodded toward the chest. "You'll find your uniform in the top drawer."

Uniform? He never said anything about her wearing a uniform. For one horrifying instant she wondered if he would seize the opportunity to inflict even more humiliation by making her wear a revealing French maid's outfit. Or something even worse.

She pulled the drawer open, relieved to find a plain, drab gray, white collared dress. The same kind his mother wore when she worked for Isabelle's parents. She almost asked how he knew what size to get, but upon close inspection realized that the garment would be too big.

She slid the drawer closed and turned to face Emilio. He stood just inside the doorway, arms folded, expression dark—an overwhelming presence in the modest space. And he was blocking the door.

She felt a quick jab of alarm.

She was cornered. In a bedroom no less. What if his

intentions were less than noble? What if he'd brought her here so he could take what she'd denied him fifteen years ago?

Of course he wouldn't. Any man who would wait a year to be with a woman knew a thing or two about self-control. Besides, why would he want to have sex with someone he clearly hated? He wasn't that sort of man. At least, he never used to be.

He must have sensed her apprehension. That damned brow lifted again and he asked, with a look of amusement, "Do I frighten you, Izzie?"

Three

Izzie. Emilio was the only one who ever called her that. Hearing it again, after so many years, made Isabelle long to recapture the happiness of those days. The sense of hopefulness. The feeling that as long as they had each other, they could overcome any obstacles.

How wrong she had been. She'd discovered that there were some obstacles she would never overcome. At least, not until it was too late.

She squared her shoulders and told Emilio, "You don't scare me."

He stepped closer. "Are you sure? For a second there, I could swear you looked nervous."

She resisted the urge to take a step back. But not from fear. She just didn't appreciate him violating her personal space. She didn't like the way it made her feel. Out of control. Defenseless. His presence still did something to her after all this time. He would never know how hard it had been to tell him no back then, to wait. So many times she had come *this close* to giving in. If he had pushed a little harder, she probably would have. But he had been too much of a gentleman. A genuinely good guy. He had respected her.

Not anymore.

"I know you," she said. "You're harmless."

He moved even closer, so she had to crane her neck to look into his eyes. "Maybe I've changed."

Unlikely. And she refused to back down, to let him intimidate her.

She folded her arms and glared up at him, and after a few seconds more he backed away, then he turned and walked out. She assumed she was meant to follow him. A proper host would have given her time to unpack and freshen up. He might have offered her something to drink. But he wasn't her host. He was her employer. Or more appropriately, her warden. This was just a prison of a different kind. A prison of hurt and regret.

On the kitchen counter lay the duty list he'd mentioned. He handed it to her and when she saw that it was *eight* pages single-spaced she nearly swallowed her own tongue. Her shock must have shown, because that damned brow quirked up and Emilio asked, "Problem?"

She swallowed hard and shook her head. "None at all."

She flipped through it, seeing that it was efficiently organized by room and listed which chores should be performed on which day. Some things, like vacuuming the guest rooms and polishing the chrome in the corresponding bathrooms, were done on a weekly basis, alternating one of the five spare bedrooms every day. Other duties such as dusting the marble in the entryway and polishing the kitchen counters was a daily task. That didn't even include the cooking.

It was difficult to believe that one person could accomplish this much in one day. From the looks of it, she would be working from dawn to dusk without a break.

"I'm putting a few final touches on the menus, but you'll have them first thing tomorrow," Emilio said. "I'm assuming you can cook."

Not if it meant doing much more than heating a frozen dinner in the microwave or boiling water on a hot plate. "I'll manage."

"Of course you'll be responsible for all the shopping as well. You'll have a car at your disposal. And you're welcome to eat whatever you desire." He gave her a quick once-over, not bothering to hide his distaste. "Although from the looks of you, I'm guessing you don't eat much."

Eating required money and that was in short supply these days. She refused to sponge off her mother, whose financial situation was only slightly less grave, and no one was interested in hiring a thief six weeks from a twenty-to-life visit to the slammer. Besides, Isabelle had been such a nervous wreck lately, every time she tried to eat she would get a huge lump in her throat, through which food simply refused to pass.

She shrugged. "Like they say in Hollywood, there's no such thing as too thin."

"I see you still have the same irrational hang-ups about your body," he snapped back, his contempt so thick she could have choked on it. "I remember that you would only undress in the dark and hide under the covers when I turned the light on."

Her only hang-up had been with letting Emilio see the scars and bruises. He would have wanted an explanation, and she knew that if she'd told him the truth, something bad would happen. She'd done it to protect him and he was throwing it back in her face.

If this was a preview of what she should expect from the next thirty days, it would be a long month. But she could take it. And the less she said, the better.

The fact that she remained silent, that she didn't rise to her own defense, seemed to puzzle him. She waited for his next attack, but instead he gestured her out of the kitchen. "The living room is this way."

If he had more barbs to throw, he was saving them for another time.

She could hardly wait.

Though Emilio's hospitality left a lot to be desired, his home had all the comforts a person could possibly need. Six bedrooms and eight baths, a state of the art media room and a fitness/game room complete with autographed sports memorabilia. He had a penchant for Mexican pottery and an art collection so vast he could open a gallery. The house was furnished and decorated with a lively, southwestern flair.

It was as close to perfect as a home could be, the apotheosis of his ambitions, yet for some reason it seemed…empty. Perfect to the point of feeling almost unoccupied. Or maybe it simply lacked a woman's touch.

When they got to the master suite he stopped outside the door. "This room is off-limits. The same goes for my office downstairs."

Fine with her. That much less work as far as she was concerned. Besides, his bedroom was the last place she wanted to be spending any time.

He ended the tour there, and they walked back down to the kitchen. "Be sure you study that list, as I expect you to adhere to those exact specifications."

Her work would be exemplary. Now that she'd had a taste of how bitter he was, it was essential that she not give him a single reason to find fault with her performance. Too much was at stake. "If there's nothing more, I'll go to my room now," she said.

"No need to rush off." He peeled off his jacket and tossed it over the back of a kitchen chair. Underneath he wore a form-fitting muscle shirt that accentuated every plane of lean muscle in his chest and abs, and she was far from immune to the physical draw of an attractive man. Especially one she had never completely fallen out of love with. Meaning the less time she spent with him, the better.

He grabbed a bottled water from the fridge, but didn't offer her one. "It's early. Stick around for a while."

"I'm tired," she told him. "And I need to study that list."

"But we haven't had a chance to catch up." He propped himself against the counter, as though he was settling in for a friendly chat. "What have you been up to the past fifteen years? Besides defrauding the better part of Texas high society."

She bit the inside of her cheek.

"You know what I find ironic? I'll bet if your parents had to guess who they thought was more likely to go to federal prison, you or me, they would have chosen the son of Cuban immigrants over their precious daughter."

Apparently his idea of catching up would consist of thinly veiled insults and jabs at her character. *Swell.*

"No opinion?" he asked, clearly hoping she would retaliate, but she refused to be baited. Others had said much worse and she'd managed to ignore them, too. Reporters and law officials, although the worst of it had come from people who had supposedly been her friends. But she wouldn't begrudge a single one of them their very strong opinions. Even if the only thing she was truly guilty of was stupidity.

"It's just as well," Emilio said. "I have work to catch up on."

Struggling to keep her face devoid of emotion so he wouldn't see how relieved she was, she grabbed the list and walked to her quarters, ultra-aware of his gaze boring into her back. Once inside she closed the door and leaned against it. She hadn't been lying, she was truly exhausted. She couldn't recall the last time she'd had a decent night's sleep.

She gazed longingly at the bed, but it was still early, and she had to at least make an effort to familiarize herself with her duties before she succumbed to exhaustion.

She hung her sweater on the back of the folding chair and sat down, setting the list in front of her on the desk.

According to the housekeeper's schedule, Emilio's car picked him up at seven-thirty sharp, so Isabelle had to be up no later than six-thirty to fix his coffee and make his breakfast. If she was in bed by ten, she would get a solid eight and a half hours' sleep. About double what she'd been getting at the motel if she counted all the times she was jolted awake by strange noises. The idea of feeling safe and secure while she slept was an enticing one, as was the anticipation of eating something other than ramen noodles for breakfast, lunch and dinner.

If she could manage to avoid Emilio, staying here might not be so bad after all.

Usually Emilio slept like a baby, but knowing he wasn't alone in the house had him tossing and turning most of the night.

It had been odd, after so many years apart, to see Isabelle standing on his front porch waiting for him. After she married Betts, Emilio had intended never to cross paths with her again. He'd declined invitations to functions that he knew she would be attending and chose his friends and acquaintances with the utmost care.

He had done everything in his power to avoid her, yet here she was, sleeping in his servants' quarters. Maybe the pool house would have been a better alternative.

He stared through the dark at the ceiling, recalling their exchange of words earlier. Isabelle had changed. She used to be so subdued and timid. She would have recoiled from his angry words and cowered in the face of his resentment, and she never would have dished out any caustic comments of her own. A life of crime must have hardened her.

But what had Alejandro said? She was guilty on paper, but there had been new developments. Could she be innocent?

That didn't change what she had done to him, and what her father had done to Emilio's family. She could have implored him to keep his mother on as an employee, or to at least give her a positive recommendation. She hadn't even tried.

In a way, he wished he had never met her. But according to her, it was destiny. She used to say she knew from the first moment she laid eyes on him that they were meant to be with one another, that fate had drawn them together. Although technically he had known her for years before he'd ever really noticed her. His mother drove them to school in the mornings, he and his brothers to public school and Izzie to the private girls' school down the road, and other than an occasional "hi," she barely spoke to him. To him, she had never been more than the daughter of his mother's employer, a girl too conceited to give him the time of day. Only later had she admitted that she'd had such a crush on him that she'd been too tongue-tied to speak.

During his junior year of high school he'd gotten his own car and rarely saw her after that. Then, when he was in college, she had shown up out of the blue at the house he'd rented on campus for the summer session. She had just graduated from high school and planned to attend classes there in the fall. She asked if he would show her around campus.

Though it seemed an odd request considering they had barely ever spoken, he felt obligated, since her parents paid his mother's salary. They spent the afternoon together, walking and chatting, and in those few hours he began to see a side of her that he hadn't known existed. She was intelligent and witty, but with a childlike innocence he found compelling. He realized that what he had once mistaken for conceit and entitlement was really shyness and self-doubt. He found that he could open up to her, that despite their vast social differences, she understood him. He liked her, and there was no doubt she had romantic feelings toward him, but she was young and naive and he knew her parents would never approve of their daughter dating the son of the hired help. He decided that they could be friends, but nothing more.

Then she kissed him.

He had walked her back to her car and they were saying goodbye. Without warning she threw her arms around his neck and pressed her lips to his. He was stunned—and aroused—and though he knew he should stop her, the scent of her skin and the taste of her lips were irresistible. They stood there in the dark kissing for a long time, until she said she had to get home. But by then it was too late. He was hooked.

He spent every minute he wasn't at work or in class that summer with her, and when they were apart it was torture. They were only dating two weeks when he told her he loved her, and after a month he knew he wanted to marry her, but he waited until their six month anniversary to ask her formally.

They figured that if they both saved money until the

end of the school year they would have enough to get a small place together, then they would elope. He warned her it would be tight for a while, maybe even years, until he established his career. She swore it didn't matter as long as they were together.

But in the end it *had* mattered.

Emilio let out an exasperated sigh and looked at the clock. Two-thirty. If he lay here rehashing his mistakes he was never going to get to sleep. These were issues he'd resolved a long time ago. Or so he'd thought.

Maybe bringing Isabelle into his home had been a bad idea. Was revenge really worth a month of sleepless nights? He just had to remind himself how well he would sleep when his family was vindicated.

Emilio eventually drifted off to sleep, then roused again at four-fifteen wide-awake. After an unsuccessful half hour of trying to fall back to sleep, he got out of bed and went down to his office. He worked for a while, then spent an hour in the fitness room before going upstairs to get ready for work. He came back down at seven, expecting his coffee and breakfast to be waiting for him, but the kitchen was dark.

He shook his head, disappointed, but not surprised. His new housekeeper was not off to a good start. Her first day on the job could very well be her last.

He walked back to her quarters and raised his hand to knock, then noticed the door wasn't latched. With his foot he gave it a gentle shove and it creaked open. He expected to find Isabelle curled up in bed. Instead she sat slumped over at the desk, head resting on her arms, sound asleep. She was still wearing the clothes from last night, and on the desk, under her arms, lay the list of her duties. Her bag sat open but unpacked on the bed, and the covers hadn't been disturbed.

She must have dozed off shortly after going to her room, and she must have been pretty exhausted to sleep in such an awkward position all night.

He sighed and shook his head. At least one of them had gotten a good night's rest.

A part of him wanted to be angry with her, wanted to send her packing for neglecting her duties, but he had the feeling this had been an unintentional oversight. He would give her the benefit of the doubt. Just this once. But he wouldn't deny himself the pleasure of giving her a hard time about it.

Four

"Isabelle!"

Isabelle shot up with such force she nearly flung the chair over, blinking furiously, trying to get her bearings. She saw Emilio standing in the doorway and her eyes went wide. "Wh-what time is it?"

"Three minutes after seven." He folded his arms, kept his mouth in a grim line. "Were you expecting breakfast in bed?"

Her skin paled. "I was going to set the alarm on my phone. I must have fallen asleep before I had the chance."

"And you consider that a valid excuse for neglecting your duties?"

"No, you're right. I screwed up." She squared her shoulders and rose stiffly from the chair. "I'll pack my things and be out of here before you leave from work."

For a second he thought she was playing the sympathy

card, but she wore a look of resigned hopelessness that said she seriously expected him to terminate their agreement.

He probably should have, but if he let her go now he would be denying himself the pleasure of breaking her. Lucky for her, he was feeling generous this morning. "If you leave, who will make my coffee?"

She gazed up at him with hope in her eyes. "Does that mean you're giving me a second chance?"

"Don't let it happen again. Next time I won't be so forgiving."

"I won't, I promise." She looked over at the dresser. "My uniform—"

"Coffee first."

"What about breakfast?"

"No time. I only have twenty-five minutes until the company car is here to pick me up."

"Sorry." She edged past him through the door and scurried to the kitchen.

He went to his office to put the necessary paperwork in his briefcase, and when he walked back into the kitchen several minutes later the coffee was brewed. Isabelle wasn't there, so he grabbed a travel mug and filled it himself. He took a sip, surprised to realize that it was actually good. A little stronger than his housekeeper, Mrs. Medina, usually made it, but he liked it.

Isabelle emerged from her room a minute later wearing her uniform. He looked her up and down and frowned. The oversize garment hung on her, accentuating her skeletal physique. "It's too big."

She shrugged. "It's okay."

It was an old uniform a former employee had left so he hadn't really expected it to fit. "You'll need a new one."

"It's only for thirty days. It's fine."

"It is not *fine*. It looks terrible. Tell me what size you wear and I'll have a new one sent to the house."

She chewed her lip, avoiding his gaze.

"Are you going to tell me, or should I guess?"

"I'm not exactly sure. I've lost weight recently."

"So tell me your weight and height and they can send over the appropriate size."

"I'm five foot four."

"And...?"

She looked at the floor.

"Your weight, Isabelle?"

She shrugged.

"You don't know how much you weigh?"

"I don't own a scale."

He sighed. Why did she have to make everything so difficult?

"Fitness room," he said, gesturing to the doorway. "I have a scale in there."

She reluctantly followed him and was even less enthusiastic about getting on the digital scale. As she stepped on she averted her eyes.

The number that popped up was nothing short of disturbing. "Considering your height, you have to be at least fifteen or twenty pounds underweight."

Isabelle glanced at the display, and if her grimace was any indication, she was equally unsettled by the number. Not the reaction he would have expected from someone with a "there's no such thing as too thin" dictum.

"Am I correct in assuming this weight loss wasn't intentional?" he asked.

She nodded.

It hadn't occurred to him before, but what if there was something wrong with her? "Are you ill?"

She stepped down off the scale. "It's been a stressful couple of months."

"That's no excuse to neglect your health. While you're here I expect you to eat three meals a day, and I intend to make you climb on that scale daily until you've gained at least fifteen pounds."

Her eyes rounded with surprise.

"Is that a problem?" he asked.

For an instant she looked as though she would argue, then she pulled her lip between her teeth and shook her head.

"Good." He looked at his watch. "I have to go. I'll be home at six-thirty. I expect dinner to be ready no later than seven."

"Yes, sir."

There was a note of ambivalence in her tone, but he let it slide. The subject of her weight was clearly a touchy one. A fact he planned to exploit. And he had the distinct feeling there was more to the story than she would admit. Just one more piece to this puzzle of a woman who he thought he knew, but wasn't at all what he had expected.

Though Isabelle wasn't sure what her father had paid Emilio's mother, she was positive it wasn't close to enough.

She never imagined taking care of a house could be so exhausting. The dusting alone had taken nearly three hours, and she'd spent another two and a half on the windows and mirrors on the first floor. Both tasks had required more bending and stretching than any yoga class she'd ever attended, and she'd climbed the stairs so many times her legs felt limp.

Worse than the physical exhaustion was how inept she was at using the most basic of household appliances. It had taken her ten minutes to find the "on" switch on the vacuum, and one frayed corner on the upstairs runner to learn that the carpet setting didn't work well for fringed rugs. They got sucked up into the spinny thing inside and ripped off. She just hoped that Emilio didn't notice. She would have to figure out some way to pay to get it fixed. And soon.

Probably her most puzzling dilemma was the cupboard full of solutions, waxes and paraphernalia she was supposed to use in her duties. Never had she imagined there were so many different types of cleaning products. She spent an hour reading the labels, trying to determine which suited her various tasks, which put her even further behind in her duties.

Her new uniforms arrived at three-thirty by messenger. Emilio had ordered four in two different sizes, probably to accommodate the weight he was expecting her to gain. The smallest size fit perfectly and was far less unflattering than the oversize version. In fact, it fit better and looked nicer than most of the street clothes she currently owned. Too bad it didn't contain magic powers that made her at least a little less inept at her duties.

When she heard Emilio come through the front door at six-thirty, she hadn't even started on the upstairs guest room yet. She steeled herself for his latest round of insults and jabs and as he stepped into the kitchen, travel cup in one hand, his briefcase in the other, her heart sailed up into her throat. He looked exhausted and rumpled in a sexy way.

He set his cup in the sink. Though she was probably inviting trouble, she asked, "How was work?"

"Long, and unproductive," he said, loosening his tie. "How was your day?"

A civilized response? Whoa. She hadn't expected that. "It was…good."

"I see you haven't burned the house down. That's promising."

So much for being civil.

"I'm going to go change," he said. "I trust dinner will be ready on time."

"Of course." At least she hoped so. It had taken her a bit longer to assemble the chicken dish than she'd anticipated, so to save cooking time, she'd raised the oven heat by one hundred degrees.

He gave her a dismissive nod, then left the room. She heard the heavy thud of his footsteps as he climbed the stairs. With any luck he wouldn't look down.

A minute passed, and she began to think that she was safe, then he thundered from the upstairs hallway, "Isabelle!"

Shoot.

It was still possible it wasn't the rug he was upset about. Maybe he'd checked the guest room and saw that she hadn't cleaned it yet. She walked to the stairs, climbing them slowly, her hopes plummeting when she reached the top and saw him standing with his arms folded, lips thinned, looking at the corner of the runner.

"Is there something you need to tell me?" he asked.

It figured that he would ignore all the things she had done right and focus in on the one thing she had done wrong. "The vacuum ate your rug."

"It *ate* it?"

"I had it on the wrong setting. I take full responsibility." As if it could somehow *not* be her fault.

"Why didn't you mention this when I asked how your day went?"

"I forgot?"

One dark brow rose. "Is that a question?"

She took a deep breath and blew it out. "Okay, I was hoping you wouldn't notice."

"I notice *everything.*"

Apparently. "I'll pay for the damage."

"How?"

Good question. "I'll figure something out."

She expected him to push the issue, but he didn't.

"Is there anything else you've neglected to mention?"

Nothing she hadn't managed to fix, unless she counted the plastic container she'd melted in the microwave, but he would never notice that.

She shook her head.

Emilio studied her, as if he were sizing her up, and she felt herself withering under his scrutiny.

"That's better," he said.

She blinked. "Better?"

"The uniform. It actually fits."

Did he just compliment her? Albeit in a backhanded, slightly rude way. But it was a start.

"You ate today?" he asked.

"Twice." For breakfast she'd made herself fried eggs swimming in butter with rye toast slathered in jam and for lunch she'd heated a can of clam chowder. It had been heavenly.

He looked down at the rug again. "This will have to be rebound."

"I'll take care of it first thing tomorrow."

"Let me know how much it will be and I'll write a check."

"I'll pay you back a soon as I can." She wondered what the hourly wage was to make license plates.

"Yes, you will." He turned and walked into his bedroom, shutting the door.

Isabelle blew out a relieved breath. That hadn't gone

nearly as bad as she'd expected. With any hope, dinner would be a smashing success and he would be so pleased he would forget all about the rug.

Though she had the sneaking suspicion that if it was the most amazing meal he'd ever tasted, he would complain on principle.

Dinner was a culinary catastrophe.

She served him overcooked, leathery chicken in lumpy white sauce with a side of scorched rice pilaf and a bowl of wilted salad swimming in dressing. He wouldn't feed it to his dog—if he had one. But what had Emilio expected from someone who had probably never cooked a meal in her entire life?

Isabelle hadn't stuck around to witness the aftermath. She'd fixed his plate, then vanished. He'd come downstairs to find it sitting on the dining room table accompanied by a highball glass *full* of scotch. Maybe she thought that if she got him good and toasted, he wouldn't notice the disastrous meal.

He carried his plate to the kitchen and dumped the contents in the trash, then fixed himself a peanut butter and jelly sandwich and ate standing at the kitchen sink. Which he noted was a disaster area. Considering all the dirty pots and pans and dishes, it looked as though she'd prepared a ten course meal. He hoped she planned to come out of hiding and clean it up.

As he was walking to his office, drink in hand, he heard the hum of the vacuum upstairs. Why the hell was she cleaning at seven-thirty in the evening?

He climbed the stairs and followed the sound to the first guest bedroom. Her back was to him as she vacuumed around the queen-size bed. He leaned in the doorway and watched her. The new uniform was a major improvement, but she still looked painfully thin. She had always been finely boned and willowy, but now she looked downright scrawny.

But still beautiful. He used to love watching her, even if she was doing nothing more than sitting on his bed doing her class work. He never got tired of looking at her. Even now she possessed a poise and grace that was almost hypnotizing.

She turned to do the opposite side of the bed and when she saw him standing there she jolted with alarm. She hit the Off switch.

"Surprised to see me?" he asked.

She looked exhausted. "Did you need something?"

"I just thought you'd like to know that it didn't work."

She frowned. "What didn't work?"

"Your attempt to poison me."

He could see that he'd hurt her feelings, but she lifted her chin in defiance and said, "Well, you can't blame a girl for trying. Besides, now that I think about it, smothering you in your sleep will be so much more fun."

He nearly cracked a smile. "Is that why you're trying to incapacitate me with excessive amounts of scotch?"

She shrugged. "It's always easier when they don't fight back."

She'd always had a wry sense of humor. He just hadn't expected her to exercise it. Unless she wasn't joking. It might not be a bad idea to lock his bedroom door. Just in case.

"Why are you up here cleaning?" he asked.

She looked at him funny, as though she thought it was a trick question. "Because that's what you brought me here to do?"

"What I mean is, shouldn't you be finished for the day?"

"Maybe I should be, but I'm not."

It probably wasn't helping that he'd instructed Mrs. Medina to toss in a few extra tasks on top of her regular duties, though he hadn't anticipated it taking Isabelle quite this long. He'd just wanted to keep her busy during the day. Apparently it had worked. A little *too* well.

"I have work to do and the noise is distracting," he told her.

She had this look, like she wanted to say something snotty or sarcastic, but she restrained herself. "I'll try to keep the noise down."

"See that you do. And I hope you're planning to clean the kitchen. It's a mess."

He could tell she was exasperated but struggling to suppress it. "It's on my list."

He wondered what it would take to make her explode. How far he would have to push. In all the time they were together, he'd never once seen her lose her temper. Whenever they came close to having a disagreement she would just…shut down. He'd always wondered what it would be like to get her good and riled up.

It was an intriguing idea, but tonight he just didn't have the energy.

He turned to leave and she said, "Emilio?"

He looked back.

"I'm really sorry about dinner."

This was his chance to twist the knife, to put her in her place, but she looked so damned humble he didn't have the heart. She really was trying, holding up her end of the bargain. And he…well, hell, he was obviously going soft or something. He'd lost his killer instinct.

"Maybe tomorrow you could try something a little less complicated," he said.

"I will."

As he walked away the vacuum switched back on.

Despite a few screwups, her first day had been less of a disaster than he'd anticipated.

Emilio settled at his desk and booted his computer, and after a few minutes the vacuum went silent. About forty-five minutes later he heard her banging around in the kitchen. That continued for a good hour, then there was silence.

At eleven he shut down his computer, turned off the lights in his office and walked to the kitchen. It was back to its previous, clean state, and his travel cup was washed and sitting beside the coffeemaker. He dumped what was left of his drink down the drain, set his glass in the sink and was about to head upstairs when he noticed she'd left the laundry room light on. He walked back to switch it off and saw that Isabelle's door was open a crack and the desk lamp was on.

Maybe he should remind her to set her alarm, so he didn't have to get breakfast in the coffee shop at work again tomorrow.

He knocked lightly on her door. When she didn't answer, he eased it open. Isabelle was lying face down, spread-eagle on her bed, still dressed in her uniform, sound asleep. She hadn't even taken off her shoes. She must have dropped down and gone out like a light. At least this time she'd made it to the bed. And on the bright side, she seemed in no condition to be smothering him in his sleep.

The hem of her uniform had pulled up, giving him a nice view of the backs of her thighs. They were smooth and creamy and he couldn't help but imagine how it would feel to touch her. To lay a hand on her thigh and slide it upward, under her dress.

The sudden flash of heat in his blood, the intense pull of arousal in his groin, caught him off guard.

Despite all that had happened, he still desired her.

Maybe his body remembered what his brain had struggled to suppress. How good they had been together.

Though they had never made love, they had touched each other intimately, given each other pleasure. Isabelle hadn't done much more than kiss a boy before they began dating. She had been the most inexperienced eighteen-year-old he'd ever met, but eager to learn, and more than willing to experiment, so long as they didn't go all the way. He had respected her decision to wait until marriage to make love and admired her principles, so he hadn't pushed. Besides, it hadn't stopped them from finding other ways to satisfy their sexual urges.

One thing he never understood though was why she had been so shy about letting him see her body. Despite what he had told her yesterday, he'd never believed it had anything to do with vanity. Quite the opposite. For reasons he'd never been able to understand, she'd had a dismally low opinion of herself.

After she left him, he began to wonder if it had all been an act to manipulate him. Maybe she hadn't been so innocent after all. To this day he wasn't sure, and he would probably never know the truth. He was long past caring either way.

He shut off the light and stepped out of her room, closing the door behind him. The lack of sleep was catching up to him. He was exhausted. What he needed was a good night's rest.

Everything would be clearer in the morning.

Five

Isabelle hated lying. Especially to her mother, but in this case she didn't have much choice. There was no way she could admit the truth.

They sat at the small kitchen table in her mother's apartment, having tea. Isabelle had been avoiding her calls for three days now, since she moved into Emilio's house, but in her mother's last message her voice had been laced with concern.

"I went by the motel but they told me you checked out. Where are you, Isabelle?"

Isabelle had no choice but to stop by her mother's apartment on her way home from the grocery store Thursday morning. Besides, she'd picked up a few things for her.

"So, your new job is a live-in position?" her mother asked.

"Room and board," Isabelle told her. "And she lets me use her car for running errands."

"What a perfect position for you." She rubbed Isabelle's arm affectionately. "You've always loved helping people."

"She still gets around well for her age, but her memory isn't great. Her kids are afraid she'll leave the stove on and burn the house down. Plus she can't drive anymore. She needs me to take her to doctor appointments."

"Well, I think it's wonderful that you're moving on with your life. I know the last few months have been difficult for you."

"They haven't been easy for you, either." And all because of Isabelle's stupidity. Not that her mother ever blamed her. She'd been duped by Lenny, too, and held him one hundred percent responsible.

"It's really not so bad. I've made a few new friends in the building and I like my job at the boutique."

Though her mother would never admit it, it had to be humiliating selling designer fashions to women she used to socialize with. But considering she had never worked a day in her life, not to mention the indictment, she had been lucky to find a job at all. Even if her salary was barely enough to get by on. It pained Isabelle that her mother had to leave the luxury of her condo to live in this dumpy little apartment. She'd endured so much pain and heartache in her life, she deserved better than this.

"This woman you work for…what did you say her name is?" her mother asked.

She hadn't. That was one part of the lie she'd forgotten about. "Mrs. Smith," she said, cringing at her lack of originality. "Mary Smith."

Why hadn't she gone with something really unique, like Jane Doe?

"Where does Mrs. Smith live?"

"Not too far from our old house."

Her brow crinkled. "Hmm, the name isn't familiar. I thought I knew everyone in that area."

"She's a very nice woman. I think you would like her."

"I'd like to meet her. Maybe I'll come by for a visit."

Crap. Wouldn't she be shocked to learn that Mrs. Smith was actually Mr. Suarez.

"I'll talk to her children and see if it's okay," Isabelle told her. She would just have to stall for the next month.

"Have you been keeping up with the news about Western Oil?" her mother asked, and Isabelle's heart stalled. Did she suspect something? Why would she bring Emilio up out of the blue like that?

"Not really," she lied. "I don't watch television."

"They showed a clip of Emilio and his partners at a press conference on the news the other day. He looks good. He's obviously done well for himself."

"I guess he has."

"Maybe you should…talk to him."

"Why?"

"I thought that maybe he would talk to his brother on your behalf."

"He wouldn't. And it wouldn't matter if he did. I'm going to prison. Nothing is going to stop that now."

"You don't know that."

"Yes, I do."

She shook her head. "Lenny would never let that happen. He may have been a thief, but he loved you."

"Lenny is dead." Even if he had intended to absolve her of guilt, he couldn't do it from the grave. It was too late.

"Something will come up. Some new evidence. Everything will be okay."

She looked so sad. Isabelle wished she could tell her

mother the truth, so at least she wouldn't have to worry about her own freedom. But she'd promised Emilio.

Isabelle glanced at her watch. "I really have to get back to work."

"Of course. Thank you for the groceries. You didn't have to do that."

"My living expenses are practically nonexistent now, and as you said, I like helping people."

She walked Isabelle to the door.

"That's a nice car," she said, gesturing to the black Saab parked in the lot.

It was, and it stuck out like a sore thumb amidst the vehicles beside it. "I'll drop by again as soon as I can."

Her mother hugged her hard and said, "I'm very proud of you, sweetheart."

The weight of Isabelle's guilt was suffocating. But she hugged her back and said, "Thanks, Mom."

Her mother waved as she drove away, and Isabelle felt a deep sense of sadness. Hardly a week passed when they didn't speak on the phone, or drop by for visits. They were all the other had anymore. What would her mother do when Isabelle went to prison? She would be all alone. And she was fooling herself if she really believed Isabelle could avoid prison. It was inevitable. Even if Emilio wanted to help her—which he obviously didn't—there was nothing he could do. According to her lawyer, the evidence against her was overwhelming.

Isabelle couldn't worry herself with that right now. If she did the dread and the fear would overwhelm her. She had a household to run. Which was going more smoothly than she had anticipated. Her latest attempts in the kitchen must not have been too awful, either, because Emilio hadn't accused her of trying to poison him since Monday, though he'd found fault with practically everything else she did.

Okay, maybe not *everything*. But when it came to his home, he was a perfectionist. Everything had its place, and God help her if she moved something, or put it away in the wrong spot. Yesterday she'd set the milk on the refrigerator shelf instead of the door and he'd blown a gasket. And yeah, a couple of times she had moved things deliberately, just for the satisfaction of annoying him. He did make it awfully easy.

Other than a few minor snafus, the housekeeping itself was getting much easier. She had settled into a routine, and some of her chores were taking half the time they had when she started. Yesterday she'd even had time to sit down with a cup of tea, put her feet up and read the paper for twenty minutes.

In fact, it was becoming almost *too* easy. And she couldn't help but wonder if the other shoe was about to drop.

Emilio stood by the window in Adam's office, listening to his colleagues discuss the accident at the refinery. OSHA had released its official report and Western Oil was being cited for negligence. According to the investigation, the explosion was triggered by a faulty gauge. Which everyone in the room knew was impossible.

That section had just come back online after several days of mandatory safety checks and equipment upgrades. It had been inspected and reinspected. It wasn't negligence, or an accident. Someone *wanted* that equipment to fail.

The question was why?

"This is ridiculous," Jordan said, slapping the report down on Adam's desk. "Those are good men. They would never let something like this happen."

"Someone is responsible," Nathan said from his seat opposite Adam's desk, which earned him a sharp look from his brother.

Somber, Adam said, "I know you trust and respect every man there, Jordan, but I think we have to come to terms with the fact that it was sabotage."

Thankfully the explosion had occurred while that section was in maintenance mode, and less than half the men who usually worked that shift were on the line. Only a dozen were hurt. But one injured man was too many as far as Emilio was concerned. Between lawsuits and OSHA fines, financially they would take a hit. Even worse was the mark on their good name. Until now they'd had a flawless safety record. Cassandra Benson, Western Oil's public relations director, had been working feverishly to put a positive spin on the situation. But their direct competitor, Birch Energy, owned by Walter Birch, had already taken advantage of the situation. Within days of the incident they released a flood of television ads, and though they didn't directly target Western Oil, the implication was clear—Birch was safe and valued their employees. Western Oil was a death trap.

Western Oil was firing back with ads boasting their innovative techniques and new alternative, environmentally friendly practices.

"I don't suppose you'll tell me how the investigation is going," Jordan said.

Adam and Nathan exchanged a look. When they agreed to launch a private investigation, it was decided that Jordan wouldn't be involved. As Chief Operations Officer he was the one closest to the workers in the refinery. They trusted him, so he needed a certain degree of deniability. A fact Jordan was clearly not happy about.

They had promised to keep him in the loop, but

privately Adam had confided in Emilio that he worried Jordan wouldn't be impartial. That he might ignore key evidence out of loyalty to the workers.

Jordan would be downright furious to know that two of the new men hired to take the place of injured workers were in reality undercover investigators. But the real thorn in Jordan's side was that Nathan was placed in charge of the investigation. That, on top of the competition for the CEO position, had thrust their occasional sibling rivalry into overdrive. Which didn't bode well for either of them. And though Emilio considered both men his friends, there had been tension since Adam announced his intention to retire.

"All I can say is that it's going slowly," Nathan told Jordan. "How is morale?"

"Tom Butler, my foreman, says the men are nervous. They know the line was thoroughly checked before the accident. Rumor is someone in the refinery is to blame for the explosion. They're not sure who to trust."

"A little suspicion could work to our advantage," Nathan said. "If the men are paying attention to one another, another act of sabotage won't be so easy."

Jordan glared at his older sibling. "Yeah, genius. Or the men will be so busy watching their coworkers they won't be paying attention to their own duties and it could cause an accident. A real one this time."

Emilio stifled a smile. Normally Jordan was the most even-tempered of the four, but this situation was turning him into a bona fide hothead.

"Does anyone have anything *constructive* to add?" Adam asked, looking over at Emilio.

"Yeah, Emilio," Jordan said. "You've been awfully quiet. What's your take on this?"

Emilio turned from the window. "You feel betrayed,

Jordan. I get that. But we *will* get to the bottom of this. It's just going to take some time."

After several more minutes of heated debate between Nathan and Jordan that ultimately got them nowhere, Adam ended the meeting and Emilio headed out for the day. He let himself in the house at six-thirty, expecting to find Izzie in the kitchen making what he hoped would be an edible meal. She'd taken his advice to heart and was trying out simpler recipes. The last two nights, dinner hadn't been gourmet by any stretch of the imagination. To call it appetizing had been an even wider stretch, but he'd choked it down.

Tonight he found two pots boiling over on the stove— one with spaghetti sauce and the other noodles—and a cutting board with partially chopped vegetables on the counter. Izzie was nowhere to be found. Perhaps she didn't grasp the concept that food could not cook itself. It required supervision.

Grumbling to himself, he jerked the burner knobs into the Off position, noting the sauce splattered all over the stove. Shedding his suit jacket, he checked her room and the laundry room, but she wasn't there, either. Then he heard a sound from upstairs and headed up.

As soon as he reached the top and saw that his bedroom door was open, his hackles rose. She knew damned well his room was off-limits.

He charged toward the door, just as she emerged. Her eyes flew open wide when she saw him. He started to ask her what the hell she thought she was doing, when he noticed the blood-soaked paper towel she was holding on her left hand.

"I'm sorry," she said. "I didn't mean to invade your privacy. I was looking for a first-aid kit. I thought it might be in your bathroom."

"What happened?"

"I slipped with the knife. It's not a big deal. I just need a bandage."

A cut that bled enough to soak through a paper towel would require more than a bandage. He reached for her hand. "Let me see."

She pulled out of his reach. "I told you, it's not a big deal. It's a small cut."

"Then it won't hurt to let me look at it." Before she could move away again, he grabbed her arm.

He lifted away the paper towels and blood oozed from a wound in the fleshy part between the second and third knuckle of her index finger. He wiped it away to get a better look. The cut may have been small, but it was deep.

So much for a relaxing night at home. He sighed and said, "Get your jacket. I'll drive you to the E.R."

She jerked her hand free. "No! I just need a bandage."

"A bandage is not going to stop the bleeding. You need stitches."

"I'll butterfly it."

"Even if that did work, you still should see a doctor. You could get an infection."

She shook her head. "I'll wash it out and use antibiotic ointment. It'll be fine."

He didn't get why she was making such a big deal about this. "This is ridiculous. I'm taking you to the hospital."

"*No,* you're not."

"Izzie, for God sakes, you need to see a doctor."

"I can't."

"*Why?*"

"Because I have no way to pay for it, okay? I don't have health insurance and I don't have money."

The rush of color to her cheeks, the way she lowered her eyes, said that admitting it to him mortified her.

He assumed she had money stashed somewhere for emergencies, but maybe that wasn't the case. Was she really that destitute?

"Since it was a work-related accident, I'll pay for it," he said.

"I'm not asking for a handout."

"You didn't ask, I offered. You hurt yourself in my home. I consider it my responsibility."

She shook her head. "No."

"Isabelle—"

"I am not going to the doctor. I just need a first-aid kit."

"Obstinado," he muttered, shaking his head. The woman completely baffled him. Why wouldn't she just accept his help? She'd had no problem sponging off her rich husband for all those years. Emilio would have expected her to jump at his offer. Had she suddenly grown a conscience? A sense of pride?

Well, he wasn't going to sit and argue while she bled all over the place. He finally threw up his hands in defeat. "Fine! But I'm wrapping it for you."

For a second he thought she might argue about that too, but she seemed to sense that his patience was wearing thin. "Fine," she replied, then grumbled under her breath, "and you call *me* stubborn."

Six

Isabelle followed Emilio through his bedroom to the bathroom and waited while he grabbed the first-aid kit from the cabinet under the sink. He pulled out the necessary supplies, then gestured her over to the sink and turned on the cold water.

"This is probably going to hurt," he told her, but as he took her hand and placed it under the flow, she didn't even flinch. He gently soaped up the area around the cut with his thumb to clean it, then grabbed a bottle of hydrogen peroxide. Holding her hand over the sink, he poured it on the wound. As it foamed up, her only reaction was a soft intake of breath, even though he knew it had to sting like hell.

He grabbed a clean towel from the cabinet and gently blotted her hand dry. It was starting to clot, so there was hope that a butterfly would be enough to stop any further bleeding if he wrapped it firmly enough. Although he still thought stitches were warranted. Without them it could leave a nasty scar.

He sat on the edge of the counter and pulled her closer, so she was standing between his knees. She didn't fight him, but it was obvious, by the tension in her stance as he spread ointment on the cut, that she was uncomfortable being close to him.

"Something wrong?" he asked, glancing up at her. "You seem...tense."

She avoided his gaze. "I'm fine."

If she were fine, why the nervous waver in her voice? "Maybe you don't like being so close to me." He lifted his eyes to hers, running his thumb across her wrist. The slight widening of her eyes, when she was trying hard not to react, made him smile. "Or maybe you do."

"I definitely don't."

Her wildly beating heart and the blush of her cheeks said otherwise. There was a physical reaction for him, as well. A pull of desire deep inside of him. Despite everything she had done, she was still a beautiful, desirable woman. And he was a man who hadn't been with a woman in several months. He just hadn't had the time for all the baggage that went along with it.

"Are you almost finished?" Isabelle asked.

"Almost." Emilio took his time, applying the butterfly then smoothing a second, larger bandage over the top to hold it in place.

"That should do it," he said, but when she tried to pull her hand free, he held on. "How about a kiss, to make it feel better?"

Her eyes widened slightly and she gave another tug. "That's really not necessary."

"I think it is." And perhaps she did, too, because she didn't try to pull away as he lifted her hand to his mouth and pressed his lips to her palm. He felt her shiver, felt her skin go hot. He kissed her palm again, then the inside of her wrist, breathing warm air against her skin. "You like that."

"Not at all."

"Your body says otherwise."

"Well, obviously it's confused."

That made him smile. "You still want me. Admit it."

"You're delusional," she said, but there was a hitch in her voice, a quiver that belied her arousal. She was hot for him.

This was going to be too easy.

Izzie gently pulled from his grasp. "I have to finish dinner."

She turned, but before she could walk away he slipped his arms around her waist and pulled her close to him. She gasped as her back pressed against his chest, her behind tucked snugly against his groin. When she felt the ridge of his erection, she froze.

He leaned close, whispered in her ear, "What's your hurry, Isabelle?"

All she had to do was tell him to stop and he would have without question, but she didn't. She stood there, unmoving, as if she were unsure of what to do. He knew in that instant she was as good as his. But not until she was begging for it. He wanted total submission. The same unconditional and unwavering devotion he had shown her fifteen years ago.

He nuzzled her neck and her head tipped to the side. He couldn't see her face, but he sensed that her eyes were closed.

"You smell delicious, Isabelle." He caught her earlobe between his teeth and she sucked in a breath. "Good enough to eat."

"We can't do this," she said, her voice uneven, her breathing shallow.

He brushed his lips against her neck. "Are you asking me to stop?"

She didn't answer.

He slid his hands up, over her rib cage, using his thumbs to caress the undersides of her breasts. They were as full and supple as they had been fifteen years ago. He wanted to unbutton her dress and slip his hands inside, touch her bare skin. Taste her.

But all in good time.

"My bed is just a few steps away," he whispered in her ear, wondering just how far she was willing to let this go. He didn't have to wait long to find out.

"Stop."

He dropped his hands and she whirled away from him, her eyes wide. "Why did you do that? You don't even like me."

A grin curled his mouth. "Because you wanted me to."

"I most certainly did not."

"We both know that isn't true, Isabelle." He pushed off the edge of the counter and rose to his feet. He could see that she wanted to run but she stood her ground. "You like it when I touch you. I know what makes you feel good."

"I'm not stupid. You don't really want me."

"I would say that all evidence points to the contrary."

Her gaze darted to his crotch, then quickly away. "I have to go finish dinner."

"Don't bother. I had a late lunch. Save the sauce for later."

"Fine."

"But that doesn't mean you should skip dinner. I want to see another pound on the scale in the morning." She had only gained two so far this week, though she swore she'd been eating three meals a day. "And take something for your hand. It's going to hurt like hell."

"I will," she said, but his concern clearly confused her.

And it was a sensation she would be experiencing a lot from now on, he thought with a smile.

Isabelle headed downstairs on unsteady legs, willing her heart to slow its frantic pace, her hands to stop trembling.

What the *hell* had she been thinking? Why had she let Emilio touch her that way? Why had she let him touch her at all? She had been perfectly capable of bandaging her own finger. She should have insisted he let her do it herself. But she foolishly believed he was doing it because he cared about her, cared that she was hurt.

When would she learn?

He didn't care about her. Not at all. He was just trying to confuse her. This was just some twisted plot for revenge.

And could she blame him? Didn't she deserve anything he could dish out? Put in his position, after the way she'd hurt him, would she have done things any differently?

She'd brought this on herself. That's what her father used to tell her, how he justified his actions. She'd spent years convincing herself that it wasn't her fault, that he was the one with the problem. What if she was wrong? What if she really had deserved it back then, and she was getting exactly what she deserved now? Maybe this was her penance for betraying Emilio.

She heard him come downstairs and braced herself for another confrontation, but he went straight to his office and shut the door.

Limp with relief, she cleaned up the mess from the unfinished meal then fixed herself a sandwich with the leftover roast beef from the night before, but she only managed to choke down a bite or two. She covered what was left with plastic wrap and put it in the fridge—if there was one thing she had learned lately, it was to not waste food—then locked herself in her room. It was still early, but she was exhausted so she changed into her pajamas and curled up in bed. Her finger had begun to throb, but it didn't come close to the ache in her heart. Maybe coming here had been a mistake. In fifteen years she hadn't figured out how to stop loving Emilio.

Maybe she never would.

"How's the finger?" Emilio asked Isabelle the next evening as he ate his spaghetti. He usually sat in the dining room, but tonight he'd insisted on sitting at the kitchen table. If that wasn't awkward enough, he kept *watching* her.

At least he hadn't complained about dinner, despite the fact that the noodles were slightly overdone and the garlic bread was a little singed around the edges. He seemed to recognize that she was trying. Or maybe he thought if he complained she might make good on her threat and smother him in his sleep.

"It's fine," she said. It still throbbed, but the ibuprofen tablets she'd been gobbling like candy all day had at least taken the sharp edge off the pain.

"We'll need to redress it."

We? As if she would let him anywhere near her after last night.

"I'll do it later," she said.

He got up to carry his plate to the sink, where she just happened to be standing, loading the dishwasher. She couldn't move away without looking like she was running from him, and she didn't want him to know he was making her nervous. He already held most of the cards in this game he'd started. And she had little doubt that it was a game.

The key was not letting him know that he was getting to her, that she even cared what he thought.

He put his plate and fork in the dishwasher. "I should check it for signs of infection."

He reached for her arm but she moved out of his grasp. "I can do it myself."

"Suit yourself," he said, wearing a cocky grin as he turned to wash his hands.

Ugh! The man was insufferable. Yet the desire to lean into him, to wrap her arms around him and breathe in his scent, to lay her cheek against his back and listen to the steady thump of his heart beating, was as strong now as it had been all those years ago. She'd spent more than half her life fantasizing about him, wishing with all her heart that they could be together, and for one perfect year he had been hers.

But she had made her choice, one that up until a few days ago, she'd learned to accept. Now her doubts had begun to resurface and she found herself rehashing the same old *what ifs*. What if she had been stronger? What if she stood up to her father instead of caving to his threats?

What if she'd at least had the courage to tell Emilio goodbye?

She had tried. She went to see him, to tell him that she had decided to marry Lenny. She knew he would never understand why, and probably never forgive her, but she owed him an explanation. Even if she could never tell him the truth.

But the instant she'd seen his face, how happy he was to see her, she'd lost her nerve and, because she couldn't bear to see him hurting, she pretended everything was okay. She hadn't stopped him when he started kissing her, when he took her hand and led her to his room. And because she couldn't bear going the rest of her life never knowing what it would be like to make love to him, she'd had every intention of giving herself to him that night.

Emilio had been the one to put on the brakes, to say not yet. He had been concerned that she would regret giving in so close to their wedding day. She hadn't had the heart, or the courage, to tell him that day would never come.

Would things have been different if she had at least told him she was leaving? For all she knew, they might have been worse. He might have talked her into telling him the truth, and that would have been a disaster.

She never expected him to forgive her—she hadn't even forgiven herself yet—but she had hoped that he would have moved on by now. It broke her heart to know how deeply she had hurt him. That after all this time he was *still* hurting. If he wasn't why would he be so hell-bent on hurting her back?

Maybe she should give him what he wanted, allow him his vengeance if that was what it would take to reconcile the past. Maybe she owed it to him—and to herself. Maybe then she could stop feeling so guilty.

After last night she could only assume he planned to use sex to get his revenge. If she slept with him, would he feel vindicated? And was she prepared to compromise her principles by having sex with a man who clearly hated her? Or did the fact that she still loved him make it okay?

Before she could consider the consequences of her actions, she stuck her hand out.

"Here," she said. "Maybe you should check it. Just in case."

He looked at her hand, then lifted his eyes to her face. There was a hint of amusement in their smoky depths. "I'm sure you can manage on your own."

Huh?

He dried his hands, then walked out of the kitchen.

She followed him. "What do you want from me, Emilio?"

He stopped just outside his office door and turned to her. "Want?"

He knew exactly what she meant. "I know I hurt you, and I'm *sorry.* Just tell me what you want me to do and I'll do it."

His stormy gaze leveled on her and suddenly she felt naked. How did he manage to do that with just a look? How did he make her feel so stripped bare?

He took a step toward her and her heart went crazy in her chest. She tried to be brave, to stand her ground, but as he moved closer, she found herself taking one step back, then another, until she hit the wall. Maybe offering herself up as the sacrificial lamb hadn't been such a hot idea, after all. Maybe she should have worked up to this just a little slower instead of jumping right into the deep end of the pool. But it was too late now.

In the past he had always been so sweet and tender, so patient with her. Now he wore a look that said he was about to eat her alive. It both terrified and thrilled her, because despite the years that had passed, deep down she still felt like the same naive, inexperienced girl. Way out of her league, yet eager to learn. And in all these years the gap seemed to widen exponentially.

Emilio braced a hand on one side of her head, leaning in, the faint whisper of his scent filling her senses—familiar, but different somehow. If she were braver she would have touched him. She *wanted* to. Instead she stood frozen, waiting for him to make the first move, wondering how far he would take this, and if she would let him. If she *should.*

Emilio dipped his head and nuzzled her cheek, his breath warm against her skin, then his lips brushed the column of her throat and Isabelle's knees went weak.

Thank goodness she had the wall to hold her steady. One kiss and she was toast. And it wasn't even a *real* kiss.

His other hand settled on the curve of her waist, the heat of his palm scorching her skin through the fabric of her uniform. She wanted to reach up and tunnel her fingers through the softness of his hair, slide her arms around his neck, pull him down and press her mouth to his. The anticipation of his lips touching hers had her trembling from the inside out.

He nipped the lobe of her ear, slid his hand upward and as his thumb grazed the underside of her breast she had to fight not to moan. Her nipples tingled and hardened. Breath quickened. She wanted to take his hand and guide it over her breast, but she kept her own hands fisted at her sides, afraid that any move she made might be the wrong one.

His lips brushed the side of her neck, her chin. This was so wrong, but she couldn't pull away. Couldn't stop him. She didn't *want* him to stop.

His lips brushed her cheek, the corner of her mouth, then finally her lips. So sweet and tender, and when his tongue skimmed hers she went limp with desire. In that instant she stopped caring that he was using her, that he didn't even like her, that to him this was just some stupid game of revenge. She didn't even care that he would probably take her fragile heart and rip it all to pieces. She was going to take what she wanted, what she needed, what she'd spent the last fifteen years *aching* for.

One minute her arms were at her sides and the next they were around his neck, fingers tunneling through his hair, and something inside Emilio seemed to snap. He shoved her backward and she gasped as he crushed her against the wall with the weight of his body. The kiss went from sweet and tender to deep and punishing so fast it stole her breath.

He cupped her behind, arched against her, and she could feel the hard length of his erection against her stomach. If not for the skirt of her dress, she would have wound her legs around his hips and ground into him. She wanted him to take her right there, in the hallway.

But as abruptly as it had begun, it was over. Emilio let go of her and backed away, leaving her stunned and confused and aching for more.

"Good night, Isabelle," he said, his voice so icy and devoid of emotion that she went cold all over. He stepped into his office and shut the door behind him and she heard the lock click into place. She had to fight not to hurl herself at it, to keep from pounding with her fists and demand he finish what he started.

She had never been so aroused, or so humiliated, in her life. She wasn't sure what sort of game he was playing, but as she sank back against the wall, struggling to make sense of what had just happened, she had the sinking feeling that it was far from over.

Damn.

Emilio closed and locked his office door and leaned against it, fighting to catch his breath, to make sense of what had just happened.

What had gone wrong?

Things had been progressing as planned. He had been in complete control. He'd had Isabelle right where he wanted her. Then everything went to hell. Their lips touched and his head started to spin, then she wrapped her arms around his neck, rubbed against him and he'd just...*lost* it.

He'd been seconds from ripping open that god-awful uniform and putting his hands on her. He had been this-close to shoving up the skirt of her dress, ripping off her panties and taking her right there in the hallway, up against the wall. He wanted her as much now as he had fifteen years ago. And putting on the brakes, denying himself the pleasure of everything she offered, had been just as damned hard.

That hadn't been part of the plan.

On the bright side, making Isabelle bend to his will, making her beg for it, was clearly not going to be a problem.

He crossed the room to the wet bar and splashed cold water on his face. This had just been a fluke. A knee-jerk reaction to the last vestiges of a long dormant sexual attraction. It was physical and nothing more. So from now on, losing control wasn't going to be an issue.

Seven

Isabelle stood at the stove fixing breakfast the next morning, reliving the nightmarish events of last night. How could she have been so stupid? So naive?

Just tell me what you want and I'll do it.

Well, she'd gotten her answer. He hadn't come right out and said it, but the implications of his actions had been crystal clear. He wanted to make her want him, get her all hot and bothered, then reject her. Simple yet effective.

Very effective.

As much as she hated it, as miserable and small as he'd made her feel, didn't she deserve this? Hadn't she more or less done the same thing to him fifteen years ago? Could she really fault him for wanting revenge?

She had gotten herself into this mess, she'd asked for his help, now she had to live with the consequences. She could try to resist him, try to pretend she didn't melt when he touched her, but she had always been a terrible liar. And honestly, she didn't have the energy to fight him.

The worst, most humiliating part was knowing that if she told him no, if she asked him to stop, he would. He would never force himself on her. He'd made that clear the other night. The problem was, she didn't *want* to tell him no.

Unlike Emilio, she couldn't switch it off and on. Her only defense was to avoid him as often as possible. And when she couldn't? Well, she would try her hardest to not make a total fool of herself again. She would try to be strong.

She would hold up her end of the bargain, and hopefully everyone would get exactly what they wanted. She just wished she didn't feel so darned edgy and out of sorts, and she knew he was going to sense it the second he saw her.

According to Mrs. Medina's "list," Emilio didn't leave for work until nine-thirty on Saturdays, so Isabelle didn't have to see him until nine when he came down for breakfast. If she timed it just right, she could feed him right when he walked into the kitchen, then hide until his ride got there.

Of course he chose that morning to come down fifteen minutes early. She was at the stove, trying not to incinerate a pan of hash brown potatoes, when he walked into the room.

"Good morning," he said, the rumble of his voice tweaking her already frayed nerves.

She took a deep breath and told herself, *You can do this.* Pasting on what she hoped was a nothing-you-do-can-hurt-me face, she turned…and whatever she had been about to say died the minute she laid eyes on him.

He wasn't wearing a suit. Or a tie. Or a shirt. Or even shoes. All he wore was a pair of black silk pajama bottoms slung low on his hips. That was it. His hair was mussed from sleep and dark stubble shadowed his jaw.

Oh boy.

Most men declined with age. They developed excess flab or a paunch or even unattractive back hair, but not Emilio. His chest was lean and well-defined, his shoulders and back smooth and tanned and he had a set of six-pack abs to die for. He was everything he had been fifteen years ago, only better.

A lot better.

Terrific.

She realized she was staring and averted her eyes. Was it her fault she hadn't seen a mostly naked man in a really long time? At least, not one who looked as good as he did.

Lenny had had the paunch, and the flab, and the back hair. Not that their relationship had ever been about sex.

Ever the dutiful housekeeper, she said, "Sit down, I'll get you coffee." Mostly she just wanted to keep him out of her half of the kitchen.

He took a seat on one of the stools at the island. She grabbed a mug from the cupboard, filled it and set it in front of him.

"Thanks."

Their eyes met and his flashed with some unidentifiable emotion. Amusement maybe? She couldn't be sure, and frankly she didn't want to know.

Make breakfast, run and hide.

She busied herself with cutting up the vegetables that would go in the omelet she planned to make, taking great care not to slice or sever any appendages. Although it was tough to keep her eyes on what she was doing when Emilio was directly in her line of vision, barely an arm's reach away, looking hotter than the Texas sun.

And he was *watching* her.

She would gather everything up and move across to the opposite counter, where her back would be to him instead, but she doubted his probing stare would be any less irritating. She diced the green onions, his gaze boring into her as he casually sipped his coffee.

"Don't you have to get ready for work?" she asked.

"You trying to get rid of me, Isabelle?"

Well, *duh.* "Just curious."

"I'm working from home today."

She suppressed a groan. Fantastic. An entire day with Emilio in the house. With any luck, he would lock himself in his office and wouldn't emerge until dinnertime. But somehow she doubted she would be so lucky. She also doubted it was a coincidence that he chose this particular day to work at home. She was sure that every move he made was calculated.

She chopped the red peppers, trying to ignore the weight of his steely gray stare.

"I want you to clean my bedroom today," he said, reaching across to the cutting board to snatch a cube of pepper.

Of course he did. "I thought it was off-limits."

"It is. Until I say it isn't."

She stopped chopping and shot him a glance.

He shrugged. "My house, my rules."

Another calculated move on his part. He was just full of surprises today. He was manipulating her and he was good at it. He knew she had absolutely no recourse.

He sipped his coffee, watching her slice the mini bella mushrooms. But he wasn't just watching. He was *studying* her. She failed to understand what was so riveting about seeing someone chop food. Which meant he was just doing it to make her uncomfortable, and it was working.

When she couldn't take it any longer, she said in her most patient tone, "Would you please stop that?"

"Stop what?"

"Watching me. It's making me nervous."

"I'm just curious to see what you're going to cut this time. The way you hold that knife, my money is on the tip of your thumb. Although I'm sure if we keep it on ice, there's a good chance they can reattach it."

She stopped cutting and glared at him.

He grinned, and for a second he looked just like the Emilio from fifteen years ago. He used to smile all the time back then. A sexy, slightly lopsided grin that never failed to make her go all gooey inside. And still did.

She preferred him when he was cranky and brooding. She had a defense for that. When he did things like smile and tease her, it was too easy to forget that it was all an act. That he was only doing it to manipulate her.

Although she hoped someday he would show her a smile that he actually meant.

"Despite what you think, I'm not totally inept," she said.

"No?"

"No."

"So the pan on the stove is supposed to be smoking like that?"

At first she thought he was just saying it to irritate her, then she remembered that she'd been frying potatoes. She spun around and saw that there actually was black smoke billowing from the pan.

"Damn it!" She darted to the stove, twisted off the flame, grabbed the handle and jerked the pan off the burner. But she jerked too hard and oil sloshed over the side. She tried to jump out of the way, but she wasn't fast enough and molten hot oil splashed down the skirt of her dress, soaking through the fabric to the top of her thigh.

She gasped at the quick and sharp sting. She barely had time to process what had happened, to react, when she felt Emilio's hands on her waist.

He lifted her off her feet and deposited her on the edge of the counter next to the sink. And he wasn't smiling anymore. "Did you burn yourself?"

"A—a little, I think."

He eased the skirt of her uniform up her thighs. So far up that she was sure he could see the crotch of her bargain bin panties, but protesting seemed silly at this point since he obviously wasn't doing it to get fresh with her. And she knew there was something seriously wrong with her when all she could think was *thank God I shaved my legs this morning.*

The middle of her right thigh had a splotchy red spot the size of a saucer and it burned like the devil.

Emilio grabbed a dish towel from the counter and soaked it with cool water, then he wrung it out and laid it against her burn. She sucked in a breath as the cold cloth hit her hot skin.

"Are you okay?" he asked, his eyes dark with concern. "Do you feel light-headed or dizzy?"

She shook her head. What she felt was mortified.

Not totally inept, huh?

She couldn't even manage fried potatoes without causing a disaster. Although, this was partially his fault. If he'd worn a damn shirt, and if he hadn't been *looking* at her, she wouldn't have been so distracted.

Emilio got a fresh towel from the drawer and made an ice pack large enough to cover the burn, while she sat there feeling like a complete idiot.

"I guess I was wrong," she said.

He lifted the towel to inspect her leg and it immediately began to sting. "About what?"

"I am inept."

"It was an accident."

Huh?

He wasn't going to rub this in her face, try to make her feel like an even bigger idiot? He wasn't going to make fun of her and call her incompetent?

Was this another trick?

"It's red, but it doesn't look like it's blistering. I think your uniform absorbed most of the heat." He laid the ice pack very gently on the burned area. The sting immediately subsided. He looked up at her. "Better?"

She nodded. With her sitting on the counter they were almost eye to eye and, for the first time that morning, she really *saw* him.

Though he looked pretty much the same as he had fifteen years ago, there were subtle signs of age. The hint of crow's-feet branded the corners of his eyes, and there were a few flecks of gray in the stubble on his chin. The line of his jaw seemed less rigid than it used to be, and the lines in his forehead had deepened.

He looked tired. Maybe what had happened at the refinery, compounded by his deal with her, was stressing him out. Maybe he hadn't been sleeping well.

Despite it all, to her he was the same Emilio. At least, her heart thought so. That was probably why it was hurting so much.

But if Emilio really hated her, would it matter that she'd hurt herself? Would he have been so quick to jump in and take care of her? Would he be standing here now holding the ice pack on her leg when she could just as easily do it herself?

He may have been hardened by life, but maybe the sweet, tender man she had fallen in love with was still in there somewhere. Maybe he would be willing to forgive her someday. Or maybe she was fooling herself.

Maybe you should tell him the truth.

At this point it would be a relief to have it all out in the open. But even if she tried, she doubted he would believe her.

"You're watching me," he said, and she realized that he'd caught her red-handed. Oh well, after last night he had to know she still had feelings for him. That she still longed for his touch.

She averted her eyes anyway. "Sorry."

"Did you know that you cursed? When you saw the pan was smoking."

Had she? It was all a bit of a blur. "I don't recall."

"You said 'damn it.' I've never heard you swear before."

She shrugged. "Maybe I didn't have anything to swear about back then."

It wasn't true. She'd had plenty to swear about. But she had been so terrified of slipping up in front of her father, it was safer to not swear at all. He expected her to be the proper Texas debutant. His perfect princess. Though she somehow always managed to fall short.

She still didn't swear very often. Old habits, she supposed. But sometimes a cuss or two would slip out.

He lifted the ice pack and looked at her leg again. "It's not blistered, so it's not that bad of a burn. How does it feel?"

"A little worse than a sunburn."

"Some aloe and a couple of ibuprofen should take care of the pain." He set the pack back on her leg. "Hold this while I go get it."

She was about to tell him that she could do it herself, but she sort of liked being pampered. He would go back to hating her soon, and lusting for revenge. She figured she might as well enjoy it while she could.

Isabelle heard his footsteps going up the stairs, then coming back down and he reappeared with a bottle of aloe and a couple of pain tablets. He got a glass down from the cupboard and filled it with water from the dispenser on the fridge. He gave her that and the tablets and she dutifully swallowed them. She assumed he would hand over the bottle of aloe so she could go in her room and apply it herself. Instead he squirted a glob in his palm and dropped the ice pack into the sink.

There was nothing overtly sexual about his actions as he spread the aloe across her burn, but her body couldn't make the distinction. She felt every touch like a lover's caress. And she wanted him. So badly.

So much for trying to resist him. He wasn't even trying to seduce her and she wanted to climb all over him.

"Why are you being so nice to me?" she asked.

He braced his hands on the edge of the counter on either side of her thighs and looked up at her. "Truthfully, Izzie, I don't know."

It was the probably the most honest thing he had said to her, and before she could even think about what she was doing, she reached up and touched his cheek. It was warm and rough.

His eyes turned stormy.

She knew this was a bad idea, that she was setting herself up to be hurt, but she couldn't stop. She wanted to touch him. She didn't care that it was all an illusion. It felt real to her, and wasn't that all that mattered? And who knows, maybe this time he wouldn't push her away.

She stroked his rough cheek, ran her thumb across his full lower lip. He breathed in deep and closed his eyes. He was holding back, gripping the edge of the countertop so hard his knuckles were white.

She knew she was playing with fire and she didn't care. This time she *wanted* to get burned.

Eight

Isabelle leaned forward and pressed a kiss to Emilio's cheek. The unique scent of his skin, the rasp of his beard stubble, was familiar and comfortable and exciting all at once. Which was probably why her heart was beating so hard and her hands were trembling. The idea that he might push her away now was terrifying, but she wanted this more than she'd ever wanted anything in her life.

She kissed the corner of his mouth, then his lips and he lost it. He wrapped his hands around her hips and tugged her to the edge of the countertop, kissing her hard. Her breasts crushed against his chest, legs went around his waist. This would be no slow, sensual tease like last night.

She had always fantasized about their first time being sweet and tender, and preferably in a bed. There would be candles and champagne and soft music playing. Now none of that seemed to matter. She wanted him with a desperation she'd never felt before. She wanted him to rip off her panties and take her right there in the kitchen, before he changed his mind.

She tunneled her fingers through his hair, fed off his mouth, his stubble rough against her chin. He slid his hands up her sides to her breasts, cupping them in his palms, capturing the tips between his fingers and pinching. She gasped and tightened her legs around him, praying silently, *Please don't stop.*

He tugged at the top button on her uniform, and when it didn't immediately come loose he ripped it open instead. The dress was ruined, anyway, so what difference did it make? And it thrilled her to know that he couldn't wait to get his hands on her.

He peeled the dress off her shoulders and down her arms, pinning them to her sides, ravaging her with kisses and bites—her shoulders and her throat and the tops of her breasts. Then he yanked down one of her bra cups, took her nipple into his mouth, sucking hard, and she almost died it felt so good.

Please, *please* don't stop.

She felt his hand on her thigh, held her breath as it moved slowly upward, the tips of his fingers brushing against the crotch of her panties...

And the doorbell rang.

Emilio cursed. She groaned. Not now, not when they were *so* close.

"Ignore it," she said.

He cursed again, dropping his head to her shoulder, breathing hard. "I can't. A courier from work is dropping off documents. I need them." He glanced at the clock on the oven display. "Although he wasn't supposed to be here until *noon*."

This was so not fair.

He backed away and she had no choice but to drop her legs from around his waist.

This was *so* not fair.

"You're going to have to get it," he said.

"Me?" Her uniform was in shambles. Ripped and stained and rumpled.

"Consider the alternative," he said, gesturing to the tent in the front of his pajama pants.

Good point.

He lifted her off the counter and set her on her feet. She wrestled her dress back up over her shoulders and tugged the skirt down over her thighs as she hurried to the door. With the button gone she would have to hold her uniform together, or give the delivery guy a special tip for his trouble.

She started to turn and Emilio caught her by the arm.

"Don't think for a second that I'm finished with you."

Oh boy. The heat in his eyes, the sizzle in his voice made her heart skip a beat. Was he going to finish what he started this time? No, what *she* had started.

The idea of what was to come made her knees weak.

The doorbell rang again and he set her loose. "Go."

She dashed through the house to the foyer, catching a glimpse of herself in the full-length mirror by the door. She cringed at her rumpled appearance, convinced that the delivery person would know immediately that she and Emilio had been fooling around. Well, so what if he did? As long as he didn't recognize her, who cared?

Holding the collar of her dress closed, she yanked the door open, expecting the person on the other side to be wearing a delivery uniform. But the man standing on Emilio's porch was dressed in faded jeans, cowboy boots and a trendy black leather jacket. His dark hair was shoulder length and slicked back from his face, and there was something vaguely familiar about him.

He blatantly took in Isabelle's wrinkled and stained uniform, the razor burn on her chin and throat, her mussed hair. One brow tipped up in a move that was eerily familiar, and he asked with blatant amusement, "Rough morning, huh?"

Emilio cursed silently when he recognized the voice of the man on the other side of the door. After three months without so much as a phone call, why did his brother have to pick now to show his face again?

Talk about a mood killer.

He just hoped like hell that Estefan didn't recognize Isabelle, or this could get ugly.

Emilio rounded the corner to the foyer and pushed his way past Isabelle, who didn't seem to know what to say.

"I've got this," he said, and noted with amusement that as she stepped back from the door, she shot a worried glance at his crotch.

"I'll go change," she said, heading for the kitchen.

"Hey, bro," Estefan said, oozing charm. "Long time no see."

He looked good, and though he didn't appear to be under the influence, he was a master at hiding his addictions. Estefan was a handsome, charming guy, which was why people caved to his requests after he let them down time and time again. But not Emilio. He'd learned his lesson.

"What do you want, Estefan?"

"You're not going to invite me inside?"

With Isabelle there? Not a chance. If he had the slightest clue what Emilio was doing, he would exploit the situation to his own benefit.

"I don't even know where you've been for the past three months. Mama has been worried sick about you."

"Not in jail, if that's what you're thinking."

No, because if he'd been arrested, Alejandro would have heard about it. But there were worse things than incarceration.

"I know you probably won't believe this, but I'm clean and sober. I have been for months."

He was right, Emilio didn't believe it. Not for a second. And even if he was, on the rare occasions he'd actually stuck with a rehab program long enough to get clean, it hadn't taken him long to fall back into his old habits.

"What do you want, Estefan?"

"Do I need a reason to see my big brother?"

Maybe not, but he always had one. Usually he needed money, or a place to crash. Occasionally both. He'd even asked to borrow Emilio's car a couple of times, because his own cars had a habit of being repossessed or totaled in accidents that were never Estefan's fault.

He wanted something. He always did.

"Unless you tell me why you're here, I'm closing the door."

The smile slipped from Estefan's face when he realized charm wasn't going to work this time. "I just want to talk to you."

"We have nothing to talk about."

"Come on, Emilio. I'm your baby brother."

"Tell me where you've been."

"Los Angeles, mostly. I was working on a business deal."

A shady one, he was sure. Most of Estefan's "business" deals involved stolen property or drugs, or any number of scams. The fact that he was a small-time criminal with a federal prosecutor for a brother was the only thing that had kept him from doing hard time.

"You're really not going to let me in?" he asked, looking wounded.

"I think I already made that clear."

"You know, I never took you for the type to do the hired help. But I also never expected to see Isabelle Winthrop working for you. Unless the maid's uniform is just some kinky game you play."

Emilio cursed under his breath.

"Did you think I wouldn't recognize her?"

He had hoped, but he should have known better.

"I don't suppose Mama knows what you're doing."

He recognized a threat when he heard one. He held the door open. "Five minutes."

With an arrogant smile, Estefan strolled in.

"Wait here," Emilio said, then walked to the kitchen. Isabelle had changed into a clean uniform and was straightening up the mess from breakfast. She'd fixed her hair and the beard burns had begun to fade.

He should have waited until he shaved to kiss her, but then, he hadn't been expecting her to make the first move. And he hadn't meant to reciprocate. So much for regaining his control. If Estefan hadn't shown up, Emilio had no doubt they would be in his bed right now. Which would have been a huge mistake.

This wasn't working out at all as he'd planned. He wasn't sure if it was his fault, or hers. All he knew was that it had to stop.

She tensed when he entered the room, looking past him to the doorway. He turned to see that his brother had followed him. Figures. Why would he expect Estefan to do anything he asked?

"It's okay," Emilio told Isabelle. "We're going to my

office to talk. I just wanted to tell you to forget about breakfast."

She nodded, then squared her shoulders and met Estefan's gaze. "Mr. Suarez."

"Ms. Winthrop," he said, the words dripping with disdain. "Shouldn't you be in prison?"

The old Isabelle would have withered from his challenge, but this Isabelle held her head high. "Five more weeks. Thanks for asking. Can I offer you something to drink?"

"He's not staying," Emilio said, gesturing Estefan to follow him. "Let's get this over with."

When they were in his office with the door closed, Estefan said, "Isabelle Winthrop, huh? I had no idea you were that hard up."

"Not that it's any of your business, but I'm not sleeping with her." Not yet, anyway. And he was beginning to think making her work as his housekeeper might have to be the extent of his revenge. There were consequences to getting close to her that he had never anticipated.

"So, what is she doing here?"

"She works for me."

"Why would you hire someone like her? After what her family did to our mother. After what she did to you."

"That's my business."

A slow smile crossed his face. "Ah, I get it. Make her work for you, the way our mother worked for her. Nice."

"I'm glad you approve."

"What does she get out of it?"

"She wants Alejandro to cut a deal for her mother, so she won't go to prison."

"So, Alejandro knows what you're doing?"

Emilio took a seat behind his desk, to keep the balance

of power clear. "Let's talk about you, Estefan. What do *you* want?"

"You assume I'm here because I want something from you?"

Emilio shot him a look, putting a chink in the arrogant facade. Estefan crossed the room to look out the window. He didn't even have the guts to look Emilio in the face. "I want you to hear me out before you say anything."

Emilio folded his arms across his chest. *Here we go.*

"There are these people, and I owe them money."

Emilio opened his mouth to say he wouldn't give him a penny, but Estefan raised a hand to stop him. "I'm not asking you for a handout. That's not why I'm here. I have the money to pay them. It's just not accessible at the moment."

"Why?"

"Someone is holding it for me."

"Who?"

"A business associate. He has to liquidate a few assets to pay me, and that's going to take several days. But these men are impatient. I just need a place to hang out until I get the funds. Somewhere they won't find me. It would only be for a few days. Thanksgiving at the latest."

Which was *five* days away. Emilio didn't want his brother around for five minutes, much less the better part of a week.

"Suppose they come looking for you here?" Emilio asked.

"Even if they did, this place is a fortress." He crossed the room, braced his hands on Emilio's desk, a desperation in his eyes that he didn't often let show. "You have to help me, Emilio. I've been trying so hard to set my life straight. After I pay this debt I'm in the clear. I have a friend in rodeo promotions who is willing to give me a job. I could start over, do things right this time."

He wanted to believe his brother, but he'd heard the same story too many times before.

Estefan must have sensed that Emilio was about to say no because he added, "I could go to Mama, and you know she would let me stay, but these are not the kind of people you want anywhere near your mother. There's no telling what they might do."

Leaving Emilio no choice but to let him stay. And Estefan knew it. Emilio should have guessed he would resort to emotional blackmail to get his way. He also suspected that if he refused, it was likely everyone would find out that Isabelle was in his home.

He rose from his chair. "Five days. If you haven't settled your debt by then, you're on your own."

Estefan embraced him. "Thank you, Emilio."

"Just so we're clear, while you're staying in my house there will be no drinking or drugs."

"I don't do that anymore. I'm clean."

"And you won't tell anyone that Isabelle is here."

"Not a soul. You have my word."

"And you will *not* give her a hard time."

Estefan raised a brow.

"My house, my rules."

He shrugged. "Whatever you say."

"I'll have Isabelle get a room ready for you."

"I have a few things to take care of. But I'll be back later tonight. Probably late."

"I'll be in bed by midnight, so if you're not back by then, you're in the pool house for the night."

"If you give me the alarm code—"

Emilio shot him a *not-in-this-lifetime* look.

He shrugged again. "I'll be back by midnight, then."

Estefan left and Emilio went to find Isabelle. She was kneeling on the kitchen floor, cleaning up the oil that spilled by the stove. Only then did he remember that she'd burned her leg, and wondered if it still hurt.

Maybe he should have considered that before he put the moves on her. Of course, he hadn't started it this time, had he? Seducing her had been the last thing on his mind.

Okay, maybe not the *last* thing…

She saw him standing there and shot to her feet. "I'm so sorry. If I had known it was him at the door—"

"I told you to answer it, Isabelle. It's not your fault."

"He won't tell anyone, will he?"

"He promised not to. He's going to be staying here for a few days. Possibly until Thanksgiving."

"Oh."

"It won't change anything. Except maybe you'll be feeding one more person."

"There are always leftovers, anyway."

"What he said to you, it was uncalled for. It won't happen again. I told him that he's not allowed to give you a hard time."

"Because you're the only one allowed to make disparaging comments?"

Something like that. Although now when he thought about saying something rude, it just made him feel like a jerk. He kept thinking about what Alejandro said, about the new developments. That she might be innocent. And even if she was involved somehow, was he so beyond reproach that he felt he had the right to judge her?

That didn't change what she had done to him, and what her father did to his family. For that she was getting exactly what she deserved.

"I'm sorry I ruined breakfast," she said. "I guess hash browns are a little out of my league."

Or maybe it was the result of him distracting her. He never would have done it if he had known she would get hurt. "So you'll make easier things from now on."

"I don't think frying potatoes would be considered complicated. I think I'm just hopeless when it comes to cooking. But thanks for taking care of me. It's been a really long time since someone has done something nice for me. Someone besides my mom, anyway."

"Your husband didn't do nice things for you?" He didn't mean to ask the question. He didn't give a flying fig what her husband did or didn't do. It just sort of popped out.

"Lenny took very good care of me," she said, an undercurrent of bitterness in her voice. "I didn't want for a single thing when I was married to him."

But she wasn't happy, her tone said.

Well, she had made her own bed. Emilio would have given her anything, *done* anything to make her happy. But that hadn't been enough for her.

Her loss.

She pulled off her gloves, wincing a bit when it jostled her bandaged finger.

"It still hurts?" he asked, and she shrugged. "Any signs of infection?"

"It's fine."

That was her standard answer. It could be black with gangrene and she would probably say it was fine. "When was the last time you changed the dressing?"

"Last night…I think."

From the condition of the bandage he would guess it was closer to the night before last. Clearly she wasn't taking care of it. He didn't want to be responsible if it got infected.

He held out his hand. "Let's see it."

She didn't even bother arguing, she just held her hand out to him. He peeled the bandage off. The cut itself had closed, but the area around it was inflamed. There's no way she could not have known it was infected. "Damn, Isabelle, are you *trying* to lose a finger?"

"I've been busy."

"Too busy to take care of yourself?" He dropped her hand. "You still have the antibiotic ointment?"

She nodded.

"Use it. I want you to put a fresh dressing on it three times a day until the infection is cleared up."

"I will. I promise."

"I need you to get one of the guest rooms ready. Preferably the one farthest from mine. Estefan will be back later tonight."

"So, he's not here?"

"He just left."

She was watching him expectantly. He wasn't sure why, but then he remembered what he'd told her when the doorbell rang, that he wasn't finished with her.

"About what happened earlier. I think it would be best if we keep things professional from now on."

"Oh," she said, her eyes filled with confusion. And rejection. He shouldn't have felt like a heel, but he did. Isn't this what he'd wanted? To get her all worked up, then reject her? Well, the plan had worked brilliantly. Even better than he'd anticipated. What he hadn't counted on was how much he would want her, too.

"Well, I had better get the room ready," she said. She paused, as though she was waiting for him to say something, and when he didn't, she walked away, leaving him feeling like the world's biggest jerk.

The last few weeks had been stressful to say the least. He would be relieved when Isabelle was gone, and the investigation at the refinery came to a close, and he was securely in the position of CEO. Life would be perfect.

So why did he have the sneaking suspicion it wouldn't be so simple?

Nine

So much for hoping Emilio might forgive her, that he still wanted her. He wanted to keep their relationship *professional*. And they had come so close this afternoon. If it hadn't been for Estefan showing up...

Oh, well. Easy come, easy go.

Clearly he didn't want Estefan knowing he was involved with someone like her. It was bad enough she was living in his house. And could she blame him for feeling that way? Aside from the fact that her father had ruined their mother's reputation, Isabelle was a criminal.

Alleged criminal, she reminded herself.

Unfortunately, now Emilio seemed to be shutting her out completely. He hadn't come out of his office all day, or said more than a word or two to her. No insults or wry observations. He'd even eaten his dinner at his desk. Just when she'd gotten used to him sitting in the kitchen making fun of her.

Isabelle loaded the last of the dinner dishes in the dishwasher and set it to run. It was only eight and all her work for the day was finished, but the idea of sitting around feeling sorry for herself on a Saturday night was depressing beyond words. Maybe it was time she paid her mom another visit. They could watch a movie or play a game of Scrabble. She could use a little cheering up, and she knew that no matter what, her mother was there for her.

If Emilio would let her go. The only way she could get there, short of making her mother come get her, or taking a cab, was to use his car. She could lie and say she was going grocery shopping, but when she came home empty-handed he would definitely be suspicious. And would he really buy her going shopping on a Saturday night? Besides, she didn't like lying.

She could just sneak out without telling him, and deal with the consequences when she got back.

Yeah, that was probably the way to go.

She changed out of her uniform, grabbed her purse and sweater and when she walked back into the kitchen for the car keys Emilio was there, getting an apple from the fridge. He looked surprised to see her in her street clothes.

Well, shoot. So much for sneaking out.

"Going somewhere?" he asked.

"I finished all my work so I thought I would go see my mother. I won't be late."

"Did Estefan get back yet?"

"Not yet."

"You're taking the Saab?"

She nodded, bracing for an argument.

"Well, then, drive safe."

Drive safe? That was *it?* Wasn't he going to give her a hard time about going out? Or say something about her taking his car for personal use? Instead he walked out of the kitchen and a few seconds later she heard his office door close.

Puzzled, she headed out to the garage, wondering what had gotten into him. Not that she liked it when he acted like an overbearing jerk. But this was just too weird.

The drive to her mother's apartment was only fifteen minutes. Her car was in the lot, and the light was on in her living room. Isabelle parked and walked to the door. She heard laughter from inside and figured that her mother was watching television. She knocked, and a few seconds later the door opened.

"Isabelle!" her mom said, clearly surprised to see her. "What are you doing here?"

"Mrs. Smith didn't need me for the night and I was bored. I thought we could watch a movie or something."

Normally her mother would invite her right in, but she stood blocking the doorway. She looked nervous. "Oh, well…now isn't a good time."

Isabelle frowned. "Is something wrong?"

"No, nothing." She glanced over her shoulder. "It's just…I have company."

Company? Though Isabelle hadn't noticed at first, her mother looked awfully well put together for a quiet night at home. Her hair was swept up and she wore a skirt and blouse that Isabelle had never seen before. She looked beautiful. But for whom?

"Adriana, who is it?" a voice asked. A *male* voice.

Her mother had a *man* over?

As far as Isabelle knew, she hadn't dated anyone since her husband died three years ago. She had serious trust issues. And who wouldn't after thirty-five years with a bastard like Isabelle's father?

But was he a boyfriend? A casual acquaintance?

Her mother blushed, and she stepped back from the door. "Come in."

Isabelle stepped into the apartment and knew immediately that this was no "friendly" social call. There were lit candles on the coffee table and an open bottle of wine with two glasses. The good crystal, Isabelle noted.

"Isabelle, this is Ben McPherson. Ben, this is my daughter."

Isabelle wasn't sure what she expected, but it sure wasn't the man who stood to greet her.

"Isabelle!" he said, reaching out to shake her hand, pumping it enthusiastically. "Good to finally meet you!"

He was big and boisterous with longish salt-and-pepper hair, dressed in jeans and a Hawaiian shirt. He looked like an ex-hippie, with a big question mark on the *ex,* and seemed to exude happiness and good nature from every pore. He was also the polar opposite of Isabelle's father.

And though she had known him a total of five seconds, Isabelle couldn't help but like him.

"Ben owns the coffee shop next to the boutique where I work," her mother said.

"Would you like to join us?" Ben asked. "We were just getting ready to pop in a movie."

The fact that she almost accepted his offer was a testament to how low her life had sunk. The last thing her mother needed was Isabelle crashing her dates. Being the third wheel was even worse than being alone.

"Maybe some other time."

"Are you sure you can't stay for a quick glass of wine?"

"Not while I'm driving. But it was very nice meeting you, Ben."

"You, too, Isabelle."

"I'll walk you to your car," her mother said, and she told Ben, "I'll be right back."

Isabelle followed her mother out the door, shutting it behind them.

"Are you upset?" her mother asked, looking worried.

"About what?"

"That I have a man friend."

"Of course not! Why would I be upset? I want you to be happy. Ben seems very nice."

A shy smile tilted her lips. "He is. I get coffee in his shop before work. He's asked me out half a dozen times, and I finally said yes."

"So you like him?"

"He still makes me a little nervous, but he's such a nice man. He knows all about the indictment, but he doesn't care."

"He sounds like a keeper." She nudged her mom and asked, "Is he a good kisser?"

"Isabelle!" she said, looking scandalized. "I haven't kissed anyone but your father since I was sixteen. To be honest, the idea is a little scary."

They got to the car and Isabelle turned to face her. "Are you physically attracted to him?"

She smiled shyly and nodded. "I think I just need to take things slow."

"And he understands that?"

"We've talked. About your father, and the way things used to be. He's such a good listener."

"How many times have you seen him?"

"This is our third date."

She'd seen him *three* times and hadn't said anything? Isabelle thought they told each other everything.

And who was she to talk when she'd told her mother she worked for the fictional Mrs. Smith?

"You're upset," her mother said, looking crestfallen.

"No, just a little surprised."

"I wanted to tell you, I was just…embarrassed, I guess. If that makes any sense. I keep thinking that he's going to figure out that I'm not such a great catch, and every date we go on will be our last."

She could thank Isabelle's dad for that. He'd put those ideas into her head.

"He's lucky to have you and I'm sure he knows it."

"He does seem to like me. He's already talking about what we'll do next weekend."

"Well, then, I'd better let you get back inside." She gave her mother a hug. "Have fun, but not *too* much fun. Although after three dates, I would seriously consider letting him kiss you."

Her mother smiled. "I will."

"I'll see you Thursday, then. Is there anything you need me to bring?"

"Oh, I was thinking…well, the thing is, my oven here isn't very reliable, and…actually, Ben invited me to Thanksgiving dinner with him and a few of his friends. I thought you could come along."

That would be beyond awkward, especially when his friends found out who she was. But she could see that her mother really wanted to go, and she wouldn't out of guilt if Isabelle didn't come up with a viable excuse.

"Mrs. Smith's family asked me to have dinner with them," she lied. "They've been so kind to me, the truth is I felt bad telling them no. So if you want to eat with Ben and his friends, that's fine."

"Are you sure? We always spend Thanksgiving together."

Not after this year, unless her mother wanted to eat at the women's correctional facility. It was good that she was making new friends, getting on with her life. To fill the void when Isabelle was gone.

She forced a smile. "I'm sure."

She gave her one last hug, then got in the car. Her mother waved as she drove off. It seemed as if she was finally getting on with her life. Isabelle wanted her to be happy, so why did she feel like dropping her head on the steering wheel and sobbing?

Probably because, for a long, long time, Isabelle and her mom had no one but each other. They were a team.

Her mother had someone else now. And who did Isabelle have? Pretty much no one.

But she was not going to feel sorry for herself, damn it. What would be the point of creating new relationships now anyway, when in five weeks she would be going to prison?

She didn't feel like going back to Emilio's yet, so instead she drove around for a while. When she reached the edge of town, she was tempted to just keep going. To drive far from here, away from her life. A place where no one knew her and she could start over.

But running away never solved anything.

It was nearly eleven when she steered the car back to Emilio's house. She parked in the garage next to his black Ferrari and headed inside, dropping her purse and sweater in her room before she walked out to the kitchen to make herself a cup of tea. She put the kettle on to boil and fished around the cupboard above the coffeemaker on her tiptoes for a box of tea bags.

"Need help?"

She felt someone lean in beside her. She looked up, expecting to find Emilio, but it was Estefan standing there.

She jerked away, feeling...violated. He was charming, and attractive—although not even close to as good-looking as Emilio—but something about him always gave her the creeps. Even when they were younger, when his mother would drive them to school, Isabelle didn't like the way he would look at her. Even though he was a few years younger, he made her nervous.

He still did. She had to dig extra deep to maintain her show-no-fear attitude.

Estefan flashed her an oily smile and held out the box of tea bags. She took it from him. "Thank you."

"No problem." He leaned against the counter and folded his arms. *Watching* her.

"Did Emilio show you to your room?" she asked, mainly because she didn't know what else to say.

"Yep. It's great place, isn't it?" He looked around the kitchen. "My brother did pretty well for himself."

"He has."

"Probably makes you regret screwing him over."

So much for Estefan not giving her a hard time. She should have anticipated this.

"It looks like you've got a pretty sweet deal going here," Estefan said.

She wondered how much Emilio had told him. From the tone of their conversation at the front door—yes, she'd eavesdropped for a minute or two—Emilio hadn't been happy to see his brother. Would he confide in someone he didn't trust? And what difference did it make?

"You get to live in his house, drive his cars, eat his food. It begs the question, what is he getting in return?"

Housekeeping and cooking. But clearly that wasn't what he meant. He seemed certain there was more to it than that. Why didn't he just come right out and call her a whore?

The kettle started to boil so she walked around the island to the stove to fix her tea. Emilio had belittled and insulted her, but that had been different somehow. Less... sinister and vindictive. She just hoped that if she didn't give him the satisfaction of a reaction, Estefan would get bored and leave her alone.

No such luck.

He stepped up behind her. So close she could almost feel his body heat. The cloying scent of his aftershave turned her stomach.

"My brother is too much of a nice guy to realize he's being used."

She had the feeling that the only one using Emilio was Estefan, but she kept her mouth shut. And as much as she would like to tell Emilio how Estefan was treating her, she would never put herself in the middle of their relationship. She would only be around a few weeks. Emilio and Estefan would be brothers for life.

She turned to walk back to her room, but Estefan was blocking her way. "Excuse me."

"You didn't say *please*."

She met his steely gaze with one of her own, and after several seconds he let her through. She forced herself to walk slowly to her room. The door didn't have a lock, so she shoved the folding chair under the doorknob—just in case. She didn't really think Estefan would get physical with her, especially with his brother in the house. But better safe than sorry.

Life at Emilio's hadn't exactly been a picnic, but it hadn't been terrible, either, and she'd always felt safe. She had the feeling that with Estefan around, those days were over.

Ten

Though he wouldn't have believed it possible, Emilio was starting to think maybe his brother really had changed this time. Good to his word, he hadn't asked Emilio for a penny. Not even gas money. He'd spent no late nights out partying and, as far as Emilio could tell, had remained sober for the three days he'd been staying there. The animosity that had been a constant thread in their relationship for as many years as Emilio could remember was gradually dissolving.

When they were growing up, Estefan had always been jealous of Emilio, coveting whatever he had. The cool after-school jobs, the stellar grades and college scholarships. He just hadn't wanted the hard work that afforded Emilio those luxuries. But now it seemed that Estefan finally got it; he'd figured out what he needed to do, and he was making a valiant effort to change.

At least, Emilio hoped so.

Though things at Western Oil were still in upheaval, and

he had work he could be doing, Emilio had spent the last couple of evenings in the media room watching ESPN with his brother. He felt as if, for the first time in their lives, he and Estefan were bonding. Acting like real brothers. Besides, spending time with him was helping Emilio keep his mind off Isabelle.

Since he told her that he wanted to keep things professional, he hadn't been able to stop thinking about her. The way she tasted when he kissed her, the softness of her skin, the feel of her body pressed against his. She was as responsive to his touch, as hot for him now, as she had been all those years ago. And now that he knew he couldn't have her, he craved her that much more. This time it had nothing to do with revenge or retribution. He just plain wanted her, and he could tell by the way she looked at him, the loneliness and longing in her eyes, that she wanted him, too. And so, apparently, could Estefan.

"She wants you, bro," Estefan said Tuesday evening after dinner, while they were watching a game Emilio had recorded over the weekend.

"Our relationship is professional," he told his brother.

"Why? You could tap that, then kick her to the curb. It would be the ultimate revenge. Use her the way she used you."

Which was exactly what Emilio had planned to do, but for some reason now, it just seemed…sleazy. Maybe he was ready to let go of the past. Maybe all this time he'd just been brooding. He wasn't the only man to ever get his heart broken. Maybe it was time he stopped making excuses, stopped attaching ulterior motives to her decision and face facts. She left him because she'd fallen in love with someone else, and it was time he stopped feeling sorry for himself and got on with his life.

"Honestly, Estefan, I think she's getting what she has

coming to her. She's widowed, broke and a month away from spending the rest of her life in prison. She's about as low as she can possibly sink, yet she's handling it with grace and dignity."

"If I didn't know better, I might think you actually *like* her."

That was part of the problem. Emilio wasn't sure how he felt about her. He didn't hate her, not anymore. But he couldn't see them ever being best pals. Or even close friends. As the saying went, fool me once, shame on you...

Once she was in prison, he doubted he would ever see her again. It wasn't as if he would be going to visit her, or sending care packages.

If she actually went to prison, that is. The new lead his brother had mentioned could prove her innocence. And if it did? Then what?

Then, nothing. Innocent or guilty, sexually compatible or not, there was nothing she could say or do that would make up for the past. Not for him, and not for his family. Even if he wanted to be with her, his family would never accept it. Especially his mother. And they came first, simple as that.

Estefan yawned and stretched. "I have an early start in the morning. I think I'll turn in."

Emilio switched off the television. "Me, too."

"By the way," Estefan said, "I talked to my business associate today. He hit a snag and it's looking like I won't get that money until a few days after Thanksgiving. I know I said I would be out of here—"

"It's okay," Emilio heard himself say. "You can stay a few extra days."

"You're sure?"

"I'm sure."

"Thanks, bro."

They said good-night and Emilio walked to the kitchen to pour himself a glass of juice to take up to bed with him. By the light of the range hood he got a glass down from the cupboard and the orange juice from the fridge. He emptied the carton, but when he tried to put it in the trash under the sink, the bag was full.

He sighed. Mrs. Medina had specifically instructed Izzie to take the kitchen trash out nightly. He couldn't help but wonder if she'd forgotten on purpose, just to annoy him. If that was the case, he was annoyed.

He considered calling her out to change it, on principle, but it was after eleven and she was usually in bed by now. Instead he pulled the bag out, tied it and put a fresh one in. He carried the full bag to the trash can in the garage, noting on his way the dim sliver of light under Isabelle's door. Her lamp was on. Either she was still awake, or she'd fallen asleep with the light on again.

He dropped the bag in the can, glancing over at the Saab. Was that a *scratch* on the bumper?

He walked over to look, and on closer inspection saw that it was just something stuck to the paint. He rubbed it clean, made a mental note to tell Isabelle to take it to the car wash the next time she was out, then headed back inside. He expected to find the kitchen empty, but Isabelle was standing in front of the open refrigerator door. She was wearing a well worn plaid flannel robe and her hair was wet.

"Midnight snack?" he asked.

She let out a startled squeak and spun around, slamming the door shut. "You scared me half to death!"

He opened his mouth to say something sarcastic when his eyes were drawn to the front of her robe and whatever he'd been about to say melted somewhere into the recesses of his brain. The robe gaped open at the collar, revealing the uppermost swell of her bare left breast. Not a huge deal normally, but in his present state of craving her, he was transfixed.

Look away, he told himself, but his eyes felt glued. All he could think about was what it felt like to cup it in his palm, her soft whimpers as he took her in his mouth and how many years he had wondered what it would be like to make love to her.

Where was his self-control?

Isabelle followed his gaze down to the front of her robe. He expected her to pull the sides together, maybe get embarrassed.

She didn't. She lifted her eyes back to his and just stood there, daring him to make a move.

Nope, not gonna do it.

Then she completely stunned him by tugging the tie loose and letting the robe fall open. It was dark, but he could see that she wasn't wearing anything underneath.

Damn.

You are not going to touch her, he told himself. But Isabelle clearly had other ideas. She walked over to him, took his hand and placed it on her breast.

Damn.

He could have pulled away, could have told her no. He *should* have. Unfortunately his hand seemed to develop a mind of its own. It cupped her breast, his thumb brushing back and forth over her nipple. Isabelle's eyes went dark with arousal.

She reached up and unfastened his belt.

If he was planning to stop her, now would be a good time, but as she undid the clasp on his slacks, he just stood there. She tugged the zipper down, slipped her hand inside…

He sucked in a breath as her hand closed around his

erection, and for the life of him he couldn't recall why he thought this was a bad idea. In fact, it seemed like a damned good idea, and if he was going to be totally honest with himself, it had been an inevitability.

But not here. Not with Estefan in the house. His bedroom wouldn't be a great idea, either.

"Your room," he said, so she took his hand and led him there.

The desk lamp was on, and he half expected her to shut it off, the way she used to. Not only did she leave the light on, but the minute the door was closed, she dropped her robe. Standing there naked, in the soft light… *Damn.* He'd never seen anything so beautiful, and he'd only had to wait fifteen years.

"You have to promise me you won't stop this time," she said, unfastening the buttons on his shirt.

Why stop? If they didn't do this now, it would just happen later. A day, or a week. But it would happen.

He took his wallet from his back pocket, pulled out a condom and handed it to her. "I promise."

Isabelle smiled and pushed his shirt off his shoulders. "You'll never know how many times I thought of you over the years."

Did you think of me when you were with him? He wanted to ask, but what if he didn't like the answer?

She pushed his pants and boxers down and he stepped out of them. "Do you know what I miss more than anything?" she said.

"What do you miss?"

"Lying in bed with you, under the covers, wrapped around each other, kissing and touching. Sometimes we were so close it was like we were one person. Do you remember?"

He did, and he missed it, too, more then she could

imagine. There had been a lot of women since Izzie, some who had lasted weeks, and a few who hung around for months, but he never felt that connection. He'd never developed the closeness with them that he'd felt with her.

She pulled back the covers on the bed and lay down. Emilio slipped in next to her, but when she tried to pull the covers up over them, he stopped her. "No covers this time. I want to look at you."

She reached up to touch his face and he realized that her hands were shaking. Could she possibly be nervous? This woman who, a few minutes ago, seemed to know exactly what she wanted and wasn't the least bit afraid to go after it?

He put his hand over hers, pressing it to his cheek. "You're trembling."

"I've just been waiting for this for a really long time."

"Are you sure you want to do this?"

"Emilio, I have never been more sure of anything in my life." She wound her arms around his neck and pulled him down, wrapped herself around him, kissed him. It was like...coming home. Everything about her was familiar. The feel of her body, the scent of her skin, her soft, breathy whimpers as he touched her.

He felt as if he was twenty-one again, lying in his bed in his rental house on campus, with their entire lives ahead of them. He remembered exactly what to do to make her writhe in ecstasy. Slow and sweet, the way he knew she liked it. He brought her to the edge of bliss and back again, building the anticipation, until she couldn't take it anymore.

"Make love to me, Emilio." She dug her fingers through his hair, kissed him hard. "I can't wait any longer."

He grabbed the condom and she watched with lust-glazed eyes as he rolled it on. The second he was finished she pulled him back down, wrapping her legs around his waist.

He centered himself over her, anticipating the blissful wet heat of that first thrust, but he was barely inside when he met with resistance. She must have been tense from the anticipation of finally making love. He couldn't deny he was a bit anxious himself. He put some weight into it and the barrier gave way. Isabelle gasped, digging her nails into his shoulders and she was *tight*. Tighter than any wife of fifteen years should be.

He eased back, looking down where their bodies were joined, stunned by what he saw. Exactly what he would have expected…if he'd just made love to a virgin.

No way. "Isabelle?"

It was obvious by her expression that she had been hoping he wouldn't figure it out. How was this even possible?

"Don't stop," she pleaded, pulling at his shoulders, trying to get him closer.

Hell no, he wasn't going to stop, but if he had known he could have at least been more gentle.

"I'm going to take it slow," he told her. Which in theory was a great plan, but as she adjusted to the feel of him inside her, she relaxed. Then "slow" didn't seem to be enough for her. She began to writhe beneath him, meeting his downward slide with a thrust of her hips. He was so lost in the feel of her body, the clench of her muscles squeezing him into euphoria, that he was running on pure instinct. When she moaned and bucked against him, her body fisting around him as she climaxed, it did him in. His only clear thought as he groaned out his release was *perfect*. But as he slowly drifted back to earth, reality hit him square between the eyes.

He and Isabelle had finally made love, after all these years, and he was her first. Exactly as it was meant to be.

So why did he feel so damned…guilty?

"You know, I must have imagined what that would be like about a thousand times over the past fifteen years," she said. "But the real thing is way better than the fantasy."

Emilio tipped her face up to his. "Izzie, why didn't you tell me?"

She didn't have to ask what he meant. She lowered her eyes. "I was embarrassed."

"Why?"

"You don't run across many thirty-four-year-old virgins."

"How is this even possible? You're young and beautiful and sexy. Your husband never wanted to…?"

"Can we not talk about it?" She was closing down, shutting him out, but he wanted answers, damn it.

"I want to know how you can be married to a man for fifteen years and never have sex with him."

She sat up and pulled the covers over her. "It's complicated."

"I'm a reasonably intelligent man, Izzie. Try me."

"We…we didn't have that kind of relationship."

"What kind of relationship did you have?"

She drew her knees up and hugged them. "I really don't want to talk about this."

"Did you love him?"

She bit her lip and looked away.

"Isabelle?"

After a long pause she said, "I…respected him."

"Is that your way of saying you were just in it for the money?"

She didn't deny it. She didn't say anything at all.

If she loved Betts, Emilio would understand her leaving

him. It sucked, but he could accept it. Knowing it was only about the money, seeing the truth on her face, knowing that she'd really been that shallow, disturbed him on too many levels to count.

"This was a mistake," he said. He pushed himself up from the bed and grabbed his pants.

"Emilio—"

"No. This never should have happened. I don't know what the hell I was thinking."

She was quiet for several seconds, and he waited to see what she would do. Would she apologize and beg him to stay? Tell him she made a horrible mistake? And would it matter if she did?

"You're right," she finally said, avoiding his gaze. "It was a mistake."

She was agreeing with him, and she was right, so why did he feel like putting his fist through the wall?

He tugged his pants on.

"So, what now?" she asked.

"Meaning what?"

"Are you going to back out on our deal?"

He grabbed his shirt from off the floor. "No, Isabelle, I won't. I keep my word. But I would really appreciate if you would stay out of my way. And I'll stay out of yours."

He was pretty sure he saw tears in her eyes as he jerked the door open and walked out. And just when he thought this night couldn't get any worse, his brother was sitting in the kitchen eating a sandwich and caught him red-handed.

Damn it.

When he saw Emilio his eyes widened, then a wry smile curled his mouth.

Emilio glared at him. "Don't say a word."

Estefan shrugged. "None of my business, bro."

Emilio wished Estefan had walked into the kitchen

before Isabelle started her stripping routine, then none of this would have happened.

But one thing he knew for damned sure, it was not going to happen again.

Eleven

This was for the best.

At least, that was what Isabelle had been trying to tell herself all day. She would rather have Emilio hate her, than fall in love and endure losing her again. That wouldn't be fair. Not to either of them. She was tired of feeling guilty for hurting him. She just wanted it to be over. For good.

She should have left things alone, should never have opened her robe, offered herself to him, but she'd figured for him it was just sex. She never imagined he might still have feelings for her, but he must have, or it wouldn't have matter if she loved Lenny or not.

She ran the vacuum across the carpet in the guest room, cringing at the memory of his stunned expression when he realized she was a virgin. She didn't know he would be able to tell. A testament to how naive and inexperienced she was. But as first times go, she was guessing it had been way above average. Everything she had ever hoped, and she couldn't regret it. She loved Emilio. She'd wanted him to be her first. As far as she was concerned, it was meant to be.

Except for the part where he stormed off mad.

When he'd asked her about Lenny, she had almost told him the truth. It had been sitting there on the tip of her tongue. Now she was relieved she hadn't. It was better that he thought the worst of her.

She turned to do the opposite side of the room, jolting with alarm when she realized Estefan was leaning in the bedroom doorway watching her.

His mere presence in the house put her on edge, but when he watched her—and he did that a lot—it gave her the creeps. When she dusted the living room he would park himself on the couch with a magazine, or if she was fixing dinner he would come in for a snack and sit at one of the island stools. Occasionally he would assault her with verbal barbs, which she generally ignored. But most of the time he just stared at her.

It was beyond unsettling.

Estefan raised the beer he was holding to his lips and took a swallow. Isabelle had distinctly heard him tell Emilio that he was clean and sober, yet the second he rolled out of bed every day, which was usually noon or later, he went straight to the fridge for a cold one.

The breakfast of champions.

It wasn't her place to tattle on Estefan, and even if she told Emilio what he was doing, she doubted he would believe her. It was also the reason she didn't tell him that she'd caught Estefan in his office going through his desk. He claimed he'd been looking for a pen, when she knew for a fact he'd been trying to get into the locked file drawer.

He was definitely up to something.

She turned off the vacuum. She knew she should keep

her mouth shut, but she couldn't help herself. "Would you care for some pretzels to go with that?"

"Funny." His greasy smile made her skin crawl. "Where are the keys for the Ferrari?"

"Why?"

"I need to borrow it."

"I have no idea. Why don't you call Emilio and ask him?"

"I don't want to bother him."

No, he knew his brother would say no, so it was easier to take it without his permission.

"I guess I'll have to take the Saab instead."

"Why don't you take your bike?"

"No gas. Unless you want to loan me twenty bucks. I'm good for it."

She glared at him. Even if she had twenty bucks she wouldn't give it to him. He shouldn't even be driving. He would be endangering not only himself, but everyone else on the road.

He shrugged. "The Saab it is, then."

It wasn't as if she could stop him. Short of calling the police and reporting him, she had no recourse. And in her experience, the police never really helped anyway.

Besides, she had enough to worry about in her own life without sticking her nose into Estefan's business.

"So, this arrangement not working out the way you planned it?" Estefan asked.

She wondered what Emilio had told him, if anything.

"Still a virgin at thirty-four." He shook his head. "Let me guess, was your husband impotent, or did you just freeze him out?"

The humiliation she felt was matched only by her anger at Emilio for telling Estefan her private business. She knew he was mad, but this was uncalled for. Was that his way of getting back at her?

Estefan flashed her that greasy smile again. "If you needed someone to take care of business, all you had to do was ask. I'm twice the man my brother is."

The thought of Estefan coming anywhere near her was nauseating. "Not if you were the last man on earth."

His expression darkened. "We'll see about that," he said, then walked away.

She wasn't sure what he meant by that, but the possibilities made her feel uneasy. He wouldn't have the nerve to try something, would he?

Tomorrow was Thanksgiving and he was supposed to be leaving. She would just have to watch her back until then.

Emilio's Thanksgiving was not going well so far.

He stood in his closet, fresh out of a shower, holding up the shirt Isabelle had just ironed for him, noting the scorch mark on the left sleeve. "This is a three hundred dollar silk shirt, Isabelle."

"I'm sorry," she said, yet she didn't really look sorry.

"I just wanted it lightly pressed. Not burned to a crisp."

"I didn't realize the iron was set so hot. I'll replace it."

"After you pay me back for the rug? And the casserole dish you broke. And the load of whites that you dyed pink. Not to mention the grocery bill that has mysteriously risen by almost twelve percent since you've been here."

"Maybe I could stay an extra week or two and work off what I owe you."

Terrific idea. But she would inevitably break something else and wind up owing him even more. Besides, he didn't want her in his house any longer than necessary. If there was any way he could get his housekeeper back today and let Isabelle go on time served, he would, but he'd promised her a month off.

He balled the shirt up and tossed it in the trash can in the corner. "It would probably be in everyone's best interest if you avoided using the iron."

She nodded.

He turned to grab a different shirt and a pair of slacks. He was about to drop his towel, when he noticed she was still standing there.

He raised a brow. "You want to watch me get dressed?"

"I wasn't sure if you were finished."

"Finished what?"

"Yelling at me."

"I wasn't *yelling*."

"Okay, disciplining me."

"If I were disciplining you, it would have involved some sort of punishment." Not that he couldn't think of a few. Putting her over his knee was one that came to mind. She could use a sound spanking. But he'd promised himself he was going to stop thinking of her in a sexual way and view her as an employee. Tough when he couldn't seem to stop picturing her naked and writhing beneath him.

"How about…chastising?" she said. "Dressing-down?"

"Exaggerate much? I was *talking* to you."

"If you say so."

Why the sudden attitude? If anyone had the right to be pissed, it was him.

"Is there anything else you need?" she asked.

"Could you tell my brother to be ready in twenty minutes?"

She saluted him and walked out.

He'd like to know what had gotten her panties in such a twist. Maybe she just didn't like the fact that he'd called her out on her marriage being a total sham. That he'd more or less made her admit she married Betts for his money. In which case she was getting exactly what she deserved.

He got dressed, slipped on his cashmere jacket and grabbed his wallet. Estefan was waiting for him in the kitchen. He wore jeans and a button-down shirt that was inappropriately open for a family holiday gathering, and the thick gold chain was downright tacky, but Emilio kept his mouth shut. Estefan was trying. He'd been on his best behavior all week.

Almost *too* good.

"Ready to go?"

"I'll bet you want to let me drive," Estefan said.

Reformed or not, he was not getting behind the wheel of a car that cost Emilio close to half a million dollars. "I'll bet I don't."

Estefan grumbled as they walked out to the garage. Emilio was about to climb in the driver's seat of the Ferrari when he glanced over at the Saab. "Son of a—"

"What's the matter?" Estefan asked.

The rear quarter panel was buckled. For a second he considered that someone had hit it while it was parked, but then he looked closer and noticed the fleck of yellow paint embedded in the black. Not car paint. More like what they used on parking barriers.

He shook his head. "Damn it!"

"Bro, go easy on her. I'm gonna bet she's used to having a driver. It's a wonder she even remembers how to drive."

He walked to the door, yanked it open and yelled, "Isabelle!"

She emerged from her room, looking exasperated. "What did I do this time?"

"Like you don't already know." He gestured her into the garage.

She stepped out. "What?"

"The *car.*"

She looked at the Saab. "What about it?

Why was she playing dumb? She knew what she did. "The other side."

She walked around, and as soon as she saw the damage her mouth fell open. "What happened?"

"Are you telling me you don't recall running into something?"

She looked from Emilio, to Estefan, then back to the car. She didn't even have the courtesy to look embarrassed for lying to him. She squared her shoulders and said, "Put it on my tab."

That was it? That was all she had to say? "You might have mentioned this."

"Why? So you could make bad driver jokes about me?"

"What the hell has gotten into you, Isabelle?"

She shrugged. "I guess I'm finally showing my true colors. Living up to your expectations. You should be happy."

She turned and walked back into the house, slamming the door behind her.

"Nice girl," Estefan said.

No, this wasn't like her at all. "Get in the car."

When they were on the road Estefan said, "Dude, she's not worth it."

He knew that, in his head. Logically, they had no future together. The trick was getting the message to his heart. The protective shell he'd built around it was beginning to crumble. He was starting to feel exposed and vulnerable, and he didn't like it.

"Make her leave," Estefan said.

"I can't do that. I gave her my word." Besides, he didn't think she had anywhere else to go.

"Dude, you don't owe her anything."

He'd promised to help her, and in his world, that still meant something. Estefan hadn't kept a promise in his entire life.

They drove the rest of the way to Alejandro's house in silence.

When they stepped through the door, the kids tackled them in the foyer, getting sticky fingerprints all over Emilio's cashmere jacket and slacks, but he didn't care.

"Kids! Give your uncles a break," Alejandro scolded, but he knew they didn't mind.

Chris, the baby, was clinging to Emilio's leg, so he hoisted him up high over his head until he squealed with delight, then gave him a big hug. Reggie, the six-year-old, tugged frantically on his jacket.

"Hey, Uncle Em! Guess what! I'm going to be big brother again!"

"Your dad told me. That's great."

"Jeez, dude," Estefan said with a laugh. "*Four* kids."

Alejandro grinned and shrugged. "Alana wanted to try for a girl. After all these years I still can't tell her no."

"I think she should make a boy," Reggie said. "I don't want a sister."

Emilio laughed and ruffled the boy's hair. "I think she'll get what she gets."

"Hey, Uncle Em, guess who's here!" Alex, the nine-year-old said, hopping excitedly.

"Alex." Alejandro shot his oldest a warning look. "It's supposed to be a surprise."

"Who's here?" Emilio asked him, and from behind him he heard someone say, "Hey, big brother."

He spun around to see his youngest brother, Enrique, standing in the kitchen doorway. He laughed and said, "What the hell are you doing here? I thought you were halfway around the world."

"Mama talked me into it and Alejandro bought my ticket." He hugged Emilio, then Estefan.

"You look great," Estefan told him. "But I'll bet Mama's not very happy about the long hair and goatee."

"She's not," their mama said from the kitchen doorway, hands on her hips, apron tied around her slim waist. She was a youthful fifty-eight, considering the hard life she'd lived. First growing up in the slums of Cuba, then losing her husband so young and raising four boys alone.

"He does look a little scruffy," Alana teased, joining them in the foyer.

"But I finally have all my boys together," their mama said. "And that's all that matters."

Emilio gave his sister-in-law a hug and kiss. "Congratulations, sis."

She grinned. "I'm crazy, right? In this family I'm probably more likely to give birth to conjoined twins than a girl."

Emilio shrugged. "It could happen."

"Why are we all standing around in the foyer?" Alejandro said. "Why don't we move this party to the kitchen?"

For a day that had begun so lousy, it turned out to be the best Thanksgiving in years. The food was fantastic and it was great to have the whole family together again. The best part was that his mama was so excited to have Enrique home, it took her several hours to get around to nagging Emilio about settling down.

"It's not right, you living alone in that big house," she said, as they all sat in the living room, having after dinner drinks. Except Estefan, who was on the floor wrestling with the nephews. He'd been on his best behavior all day.

"I like living alone," Emilio told her. "And if I ever feel the need to have kids, I can just borrow Alejandro's."

"You need to fill it with niños of your own," she said sternly.

"Why don't you nag Enrique about getting married?" Emilio said.

She rubbed her youngest son's arm affectionately. "He's still a baby."

Emilio laughed. "So what does that make me? An old man?"

"You are pretty damn old," Enrique said, which got him plenty of laughs.

Chris climbed into Emilio's lap and hugged him, staring up at him with big brown eyes. And Emilio was thinking that maybe having a kid or two wouldn't be so bad, just as Chris threw up all down the front of his shirt.

"Oh, sweetie!" Alana charged over, sweeping him up off Emilio's lap. "Emilio, I'm so sorry!"

"It's okay," Emilio said, using the tissues his brother handed him to clean himself up.

"Honey, take your brother up and get him a clean shirt. You're the same size, right?"

"I'm sure I have something that will work," Alejandro said, and Emilio followed him upstairs to his bedroom.

Alejandro handed him a clean shirt and said, "While I've got you here, there's something I wanted to ask you."

He peeled off his dirty shirt and gave it to his brother. "What's up?"

"How much do you know about Isabelle's father?"

He was having such a good day, he didn't want to ruin it by thinking about Isabelle and her family. "I'm not sure what you mean. Other than the fact that he was a bastard, not too much I guess."

"Did you know he had a serious gambling problem?"

"So he was an even bigger bastard than we thought. So what?"

"He'd also had charges filed against him."

"For what?"

"Domestic abuse."

Emilio frowned. "Are you sure?"

"Positive. And he must have had friends in high places because I had to dig deep."

Emilio shrugged into the shirt and buttoned it. It was slightly large, but at least it didn't smell like puke. "So he was an even *bigger* bastard."

"There's something else." His grim expression said Emilio probably wasn't going to like this. "There were also allegations of child abuse."

Emilio's pulse skipped. Had Izzie been abused? "Allegations? Was there ever any proof?"

"He was never charged. I just thought you would want to know."

"Can you dig deeper?"

"I could, if it were relevant to my case."

"Are you suggesting I should investigate this further?"

Alejandro shrugged. "That would be a conflict of interest. Although I can say that if it were me, I would try to get a hold of medical records."

"Could this exonerate her?"

"I'm not at liberty to say."

"Damn it, Alejandro."

He sighed. "Probably not, but it might be relevant in her defense."

"I thought she was taking a plea."

"She is, on the advice of counsel, and I think we've already established that she may not be getting the best advice."

So in other words, Alejandro wanted him to dig deeper. He couldn't deny that the idea she might have been mistreated was an unsettling one. He could just ask her, but if she hadn't told him by now, what were the odds she would admit it? And if she had been, wouldn't he have noticed? Or maybe it was something that happened when she was younger.

"I'll look into it."

"Let me know what you find."

He followed his brother back downstairs, but he'd lost his holiday spirit. He felt…unsettled. And not just about the possible abuse. It seemed as though quite a few things lately weren't…adding up. Like why her husband kept her in the lap of luxury and expected nothing in return, and Isabelle's sudden change of personality to Miss Snarky.

"You ready to go?" he asked Estefan an hour later.

"I think I'm going to crash here tonight. Get some quality time with the nephews."

He glanced over at Alejandro, who nodded.

His mama protested him leaving so early, so he used exhaustion from work as an excuse. Everyone knew things had been hectic since the explosion.

He said his goodbyes and headed home. When he pulled into the garage just before nine, he was surprised to find the Saab there. He figured Isabelle would have taken it to her mother's. Or maybe she thought he wouldn't want her driving it now.

He crouched down to look at the dent. He didn't doubt that it was caused by backing into something. She probably wasn't paying attention to where she was going. If she had just fessed up when it happened, it wouldn't have been a big deal. Although it wasn't like her to lie. Every time she screwed up, she owned up to it, and she had looked genuinely surprised when he pointed it out.

Curious, he walked around to the driver's side and got in. He stuck the key in and booted the navigation system, going through the history until he found what he was looking for.

Damn it. What the hell had she been thinking?

Shaking his head, he got out and let himself in the house. There was an empty wine bottle on the counter by the sink. Cheap stuff that Isabelle must have picked up at the grocery store.

He checked the dishwasher and found a dirty plate, fork, cup and pan inside. She hadn't gone to her mother's. She'd spent the holiday alone.

Twelve

Isabelle wasn't in her bedroom, so Emilio went looking for her. He found her asleep in the media room, curled up in a chair in her pajamas, another bottle of wine on the table beside her, this one three quarters empty, and beside it the case for the DVD *Steel Magnolias*. The movie whose credits were currently rolling up the screen. There was a tissue box in her lap and a dozen or so balled up on the seat and floor.

Far as he could tell, she'd spent her Thanksgiving watching chick movies, crying and drinking herself into a stupor with cheap wine.

"Isabelle." He jostled her shoulder. "Isabelle, wake up."

Her eyes fluttered open, fuzzy from sleep, and probably intoxication. "You're home."

"I'm home."

She smiled, closed her eyes and promptly fell back to sleep.

He sighed. Short of dumping a bucket of cold water over her head—which he couldn't deny was awfully tempting—he didn't think she would be waking up any time soon. He just wished she would have told him she was spending Thanksgiving alone.

And he would have…what? Invited her to his brother's? Stayed home with her and ignored his family? He wouldn't have done anything different, other than feel guilty all day.

He picked her up out of the chair and hoisted her into his arms. Her eyes fluttered open and her arms went around his neck. "Where are we going?" she asked in a sleepy voice.

"I'm taking you to bed."

"Oh, okay." Her eyes drifted closed again and her head dropped on his shoulder. He started to walk in the direction of her quarters, but the thought of leaving her in there, alone, isolated from the rest of the house in that uncomfortable little bed…he just couldn't do it.

He carried her upstairs instead, to the spare bedroom beside his room. He pulled the covers back and laid her down, unhooking her arms from around his neck. It was dark, but he could see that her eyes were open.

"Where am I?"

"The guest room. I thought you would be more comfortable here."

"I had too much to drink."

"I know."

She curled up on her side, hugging the pillow. "I don't usually drink, but I didn't think it would be so hard."

"What?"

"Being alone today."

Damn. "Why didn't you go to your mother's?"

"She wanted to be with Ben and his friends."

He had no idea who Ben was. Maybe a friend or boyfriend. "You couldn't go with her?"

"She needs to meet people, make new friends, so it won't be as bad when I'm gone."

By gone he assumed she meant in prison. So she'd spent the day alone for her mother's sake. Not the actions of a spoiled, selfish woman.

He thought about the news his brother had sprung on him tonight and wondered if it could be true, if Isabelle had been abused as a child.

He sat on the edge of the bed. "Isabelle, why didn't you tell me the truth about the car?"

"I told you why."

"What I mean is, why didn't you tell me that it wasn't you who caused the damage?"

She blinked. "Of course I did."

More lies. "I looked in the navigation history. Unless you spent the afternoon at a strip joint downtown, it was Estefan who took the car." He touched her cheek. "Why would you take the fall for him?"

Looking guilty, she shrugged. "You're brothers. I didn't want to get between you."

"You're right, we are brothers. So I know exactly what he's capable of." He brushed her hair back, tucked it behind her ear. "Is there anything else? Anything I should know?"

She gnawed her lip.

"Isabelle?"

"He's been drinking."

Emilio cursed. "How much?"

"As soon as he gets up, pretty much until you get home." She took his hand. "I'm sorry, Emilio."

"I'm disappointed, but not surprised. I've been through this too many times with him before."

"But it sucks when people let you down."

She would know.

"I have a confession to make," she said.

"About Estefan?"

She shook her head. "I ruined your shirt on purpose."

Oddly enough, his first reaction was to laugh. "Why?"

"I was mad at you. For telling Estefan that I was a virgin."

What? "I never told him that. I never told him anything about us, other than it was none of his business."

"So how did he know? He made a remark about it yesterday."

"He was in the kitchen when I walked out of your room. Maybe he heard us talking?"

"All the way from the kitchen? We weren't talking *that* loud."

She was right. He would have had to be listening at the door.

She must have reached the same conclusion, because she made a face and said, "Ew."

"He's staying at Alejandro's tonight, and tomorrow he's out of here."

"No offense, but he's always given me the creeps. Even when he was a kid. I didn't like the way he stared at me."

Then she probably wouldn't want to know that Estefan used to have a crush on her. Apparently he thought that someday they would be together, because he had been furious when he found out that Emilio was dating her. He accused Emilio of stealing her from him.

"Emilio?" she said, squeezing his hand.

"Huh?"

"I didn't marry Lenny for his money. That isn't why I left you. You can think whatever horrible things about me that you want, but don't think that. Okay?"

"I don't think you're horrible. I wanted to, but you're making it really hard not to like you."

"Don't. I don't want you to like me."

"Why?"

"Because I'm going to prison and I don't want to hurt you again. It's better if you just keep hating me."

"Do you hate me?"

"No. I *love* you," she said, like that should have been perfectly obvious. "I always have. But we can't be together. It's not fair."

He didn't even know what to say to that. How could he have ever thought she was selfish? The truth is, she hadn't changed at all. She was still the sweet girl he'd been in love with fifteen years ago. And if her leaving him really had nothing to do with Betts's money, why did she do it?

He knew if he asked her, she wouldn't tell him. He could only hope that the medical records would be the final piece to the puzzle. But there was still one thing he'd been wondering about.

"How was it your mother wound up indicted?"

"After my father died, she knew virtually nothing about finances. She didn't even know what she and my father were worth, and it was a lot less than she expected. He was heavily in debt, and nothing was in my mother's name. After the debts were paid, there wasn't much left. Lenny said he could set up a division of the company in her name. He would do the work and she would reap the benefits, only it didn't turn out that way. She's in trouble because of me."

"I fail to see how that's your fault."

"I encouraged her to sign. I trusted Lenny."

"Does she blame you?"

"Of course not. If she knew I was planning to take a plea in exchange for her freedom, she would have a fit. But my lawyer said that was the only way. She's been through enough."

Izzie's mother had always been kind to him and his brothers, and his mother never had a negative thing to say about her. If she wasn't involved, he didn't want to see her go to jail, either, but if Isabelle was innocent she shouldn't be serving herself up as the sacrificial lamb. She should be trying to fight this.

"I'm sleepy," she said, yawning.

After all that wine, who wouldn't be? "And you're probably going to have one hell of a hangover in the morning."

"Probably."

"Scoot over," he said.

"Why?"

He unbuttoned his shirt. "So I can lie down."

"But—"

"Just go to sleep." The one thing they had never done was spend the night together. He figured it was about time.

And drunk or not, he'd be damned if he was going to let her spend the rest of her Thanksgiving alone.

Isabelle woke sometime in the night with her head in a vise, in a strange room, curled up against Emilio's bare chest.

Huh?

Then she remembered that he had carried her to bed, and the conversation they'd had. Though that part was a little fuzzy. She was pretty sure the gist of it was that Emilio wasn't mad at her anymore. Which was the exact opposite of what she had wanted.

She considered getting up and going to her own bed, but she must have fallen asleep before she got the chance. The next time she woke, Emilio was gone, and someone was inside her skull with a jackhammer.

She crawled out of bed and stumbled downstairs to the kitchen. Emilio was sitting at the island dressed for work, eating a bowl of cereal. When he heard her walk in he turned. And winced.

She must have looked as bad as she felt.

"Good morning," he said.

Not. "Shoot me and put me out of my misery."

"How about some coffee and ibuprofen instead?"

Honestly, death sounded better, but she took the tablets he brought to her and choked down a few sips of coffee.

"Why are you up so early?" he asked.

"I'm supposed to be up. It's a work day."

"Not for you it isn't." He took her coffee cup and put it in the sink, then he took her by the shoulders and steered her toward the stairs. "Back to bed."

"But the house—"

"It can wait a day."

He walked her upstairs to the guest room and tucked her back into bed. "Get some sleep, and don't get up until you're feeling better. Promise?"

"Promise."

He kissed her forehead before he left.

She must have conked right out, because when she woke again, sunshine streamed in through the break in the curtains, and when she sat up she felt almost human. She looked over at the clock on the dresser and was stunned to find it was almost noon. After a cup of coffee and a slice of toast and a few more ibuprofen, she was feeling almost like her old self, so she showered, dressed in her uniform and got to work. She wouldn't have time to do all her chores, but she could make a decent dent in them.

She was polishing the marble in the foyer when Estefan came in, looking about as bad as she felt this morning.

"Rough night?" she asked.

He smirked and walked straight to the kitchen. She heard the fridge open and the rattle of a beer bottle as he pulled it out. Figures. The best thing for a hangover was more alcohol, right?

She went back to polishing, but after several minutes she got an eerie feeling and knew he was watching her.

"Is there something you needed?" she asked.

"Have you got eyes in the back of your head or something?"

She turned to him. "Are you here for your things?"

His eyes narrowed. "Why?"

She just assumed Emilio would have called him by now. Guess not.

His eyes narrowed. "What did you tell Emilio?"

She squared her shoulders. "Nothing he didn't already know."

"You told him about the car?"

"I didn't have to. He looked up the history on the GPS. He knows it was you driving."

He cursed under his breath and mumbled, "It's okay. I can fix this."

She knew she should keep her mouth shut, but she couldn't help herself. "He knows about the drinking, too, and the fact that you were listening outside my bedroom door the other night."

He cut his eyes to her, and with a look that was pure venom, tipped his half-finished beer and dumped it onto her newly polished floor.

Nice. Very mature.

He walked up the stairs to his room. Hopefully to pack.

Isabelle cleaned up the beer with paper towels then repolished the floor. She cleaned all the main floor bathrooms next, buffing the chrome fixtures and polishing the marble countertops.

When she was finished she found Estefan in the living room, booted feet up on the glass top coffee table, drinking Don Julio Real Tequila straight from the bottle.

"You're enjoying this, aren't you?" he asked. "That I have to go, and you get to stay. That once again you mean more to him than his own brother."

Once again? What was that supposed to mean?

"You're leaving him no choice, Estefan."

"What the hell do you know? Emilio and I, we're family," he said, pounding his fist to his chest. "He's supposed to stand behind me. This is all your fault."

She knew his type. Everything was always someone else's fault. He never took responsibility for his own actions.

He took another swig from the bottle. "I loved you, you know. I would have done anything to have you. Then Emilio stole you from me."

Stole her?

So in his mind they had been embroiled in some creepy love triangle? Well, that wasn't reality. Even if there had been no Emilio, she never would have been attracted to Estefan.

He shoved himself up from the couch, wavering a second before he caught his balance. "I'm tired of coming in second place. Maybe I should take what's rightfully mine."

Meaning what?

He started to walk toward her with a certain look, and every instinct she had said *run*.

First thing when he got to work, Emilio called the firm Western Oil had hired to investigate the explosion and explained what he needed.

"Medical records are privileged," the investigator told him.

"So you're saying you can't get them?"

"I can, but you can't use the information in court."

"I don't plan to."

"Give me the name."

"Isabelle Winthrop."

There was a pause. "The one indicted for fraud?"

"That's the one." There was another pause, and he heard the sound of typing. "How long will this take?"

"Hold on." There was more typing, then he said, "Let me make a call. I'll get back to you in a couple of hours."

The time passed with no word and Emilio began to get impatient. He ate lunch at his desk, then forced himself to get some work done. By three o'clock, he was past impatient and bordering on pissed. He was reaching for the phone to call the firm back when his secretary buzzed him.

"Mr. Blair would like to see you in his office."

"Tell him I'll be there in a few minutes."

"He said right now."

He blew out a breath. "Fine."

When he got there Adam's secretary was on the phone, but she waved him in.

Adam stood at the window behind his desk, his back to the door.

"You wanted to see me, boss?"

He didn't turn. "Close the door and sit down."

He shut the door and took a seat, even though he preferred to stand, wondering what he could have done to earn such a cool reception. "Something wrong, Adam?"

"You may not know this, but due to the sensitive nature of the information we receive from the investigators in regard to the refinery accident, the mail room has implicit instruction to send any correspondence directly to my office."

Oh hell.

"So," he said, turning and grabbing a thick manila envelope from his desk, "When this arrived with your name on it, it came to me."

Emilio could clearly see that the seal on top had been broken. "You opened it?"

"Yeah, I opened it. Because for all I know you were responsible for the explosion, and you were trying to reroute key information away from the investigation."

The accusation stung, but put in Adam's place, he might have thought the same thing. He never should have used the same agency. He had just assumed they would call him, at which point he would have told them to send the files to his house.

"You want to explain to me why you need medical records for Isabelle Winthrop?"

"Not really."

Adam sighed.

"It's personal."

"How personal?"

"I just...needed to know something."

He handed Emilio the file. "You needed to know if someone was using her as their own personal punching bag?"

Emilio's stomach bottomed out. He hoped that was an exaggeration.

He pulled the file out of the envelope. It was thorough. Everything was there, from the time she was born until her annual physical the previous year. He flipped slowly through the pages, realizing immediately that Adam was not exaggerating, and what he read made him physically ill.

It seemed to start when she was three years old with a dislocated shoulder. Not a common injury for a docile young girl. From there it escalated to several incidences of concussions and cracked ribs, and a head injury so severe it fractured her skull and put her in the hospital for a week. He would venture to guess that there were probably many other injuries that had gone untreated, or tended by a personal physician who was paid handsomely to keep his mouth shut.

He scraped a hand through his hair. Why hadn't anyone connected the dots? Why hadn't someone *helped* her?

What disturbed him the most, what had him on the verge of losing his breakfast, was the hospital record from fifteen years ago. That weekend had been engraved in his memory since he opened the morning paper and saw the feature announcing Isabelle and Betts's wedding. Four days earlier Isabelle had been treated for a concussion and bruised ribs from a "fall" on campus. Emilio had seen her just two days later and he hadn't had a damned clue.

In the year they had been together what else hadn't he seen?

Then he had a thought that had bile rising in his throat. He was pretty sure that last concussion and the bruised ribs were his fault.

"Son of a bitch."

"Emilio," Adam said. "What's going on?"

Emilio had forgotten Adam was standing there.

"My brother thinks she might be innocent." In fact, he was ninety-nine point nine percent sure she was. "She's… she's been staying with me the last couple of weeks."

Adam swore and shook his head. "You said you wouldn't do anything stupid."

"If she's innocent, she needs my help. That's more clear now than ever."

"Just because someone knocked her around, it doesn't mean she's not a criminal."

"If you knew her like I do, you would know she isn't capable of stealing anything."

"Sounds like your mind is already made up."

It was. And he was going to help her. He had to.

"Emilio, if it gets out to the press what you're doing—"

"It's not going to."

"And if it does? Is she worth decimating your career? Your reputation?"

He was stunned to realize that the answer to that question was yes. Because it would only be temporary, then everyone would know she didn't do it. He would spend his last penny to get to the truth if that's what it took.

"If the press gets hold of this, I'll take full responsibility. As far as I'm concerned, Western Oil is free to hang me out to dry."

"Wow. You must really care about this woman."

"I do." But what really mattered was that fifteen years ago he'd failed her. In the worst possible way. He refused to make that mistake again.

Thirteen

Emilio left work early, and when he opened the front door he heard shouting and banging.

What the hell?

He dropped his briefcase by the door, followed the sound and found Estefan outside his office. The door was closed and Estefan was pounding with his fist shouting, "Let me in, you bitch!"

"What the hell is going on?"

Estefan swung around to face him. He was breathing hard, his eyes wild with fury. "Look what she did to me!"

Deep gouges branded his right cheek. Nail marks.

"*Isabelle* did that? What happened?"

"Nothing. She just attacked me."

That didn't sound like her at all. She'd never had a violent bone in her body. "Move out of the way," he said. "I'll talk to her."

He reluctantly stepped back.

"Wait in the living room."

"But—"

"In the living room."

"Fine," he grumbled.

Emilio waited until his brother was gone, then knocked softly. "Isabelle, it's Emilio. Let me in."

There was a pause, then he heard the lock turn. He opened the door and stepped into the room, and Isabelle launched herself into his arms. She clung to him, trembling from the inside out.

"Let me look at you. Are you okay?" He held her at arm's length. Her uniform was ripped open at the collar and she had what looked liked finger impressions on her upper arms.

He didn't have to ask her what happened. It was obvious. "Son of a bitch."

"He said he was going to take what was rightfully his," she said, her voice trembling. "He was drinking again."

Son of a bitch.

"I kind of accidentally told him that you were going to make him leave. He was really mad."

"I'm going to go talk to him. I want you to go upstairs, in my bedroom, shut the door and wait for me there. Understand?"

She nodded.

If this got out of hand he wanted her somewhere safe. He watched as she dashed up the stairs, waited until he heard the bedroom door close, then walked to the living room, where his brother was pacing by the couch. "What the hell did you do, Estefan?"

Outraged, his brother said, "What did *I* do? Look at my face!"

"You forced yourself on her."

"Is that what she told you? She's a liar. Man, she *wanted* it. She's been coming on to me for days. She's a whore."

Teeth gritted, Emilio crossed the room and gave his brother a shove. Estefan staggered backward, grabbing the couch to stop his fall. He righted himself, then listed to one side, before he caught his balance.

He *was* drunk.

"What's the matter with you, Emilio?"

"What's the matter with *me?* You tried to *rape* her!"

Estefan actually laughed. "If you wanted to keep her all to yourself you should have said so."

Emilio swung, connecting solidly with Estefan's jaw. Estefan jerked back and landed on the floor.

"Emilio, what the hell!"

It took every ounce of control Emilio possessed not to beat the hell out of his brother. "You've crossed the line. Get your stuff and get out."

"You would choose that lying bitch over your own flesh and blood?"

"Isabelle has more integrity in the tip of her finger than you've ever had in your entire miserable excuse for a life."

His expression went from one of outrage to pure venom. This was the Estefan that Emilio knew. The one he had hoped he'd seen the last of. "I'll make you regret this."

Regret? He was already full of it. He thought about what might have happened if he hadn't come home early and he felt ill. What if Estefan had gotten into his office? "The only thing I regret is thinking that this time you might have changed."

"She's using you. Just like she did before."

"You know nothing, Estefan."

"I know her daddy wasn't very happy when I told him about your so-called engagement."

"You told him?"

"You should be thanking me. You were too good for her."

"You stupid son of a bitch. You have no clue what you did."

"I saved your ass, that's what I did."

He'd never wanted to hurt someone as much as he wanted to hurt Estefan right now. Instead he took a deep, calming breath and said, "Pack your things, and get out. As far as I'm concerned, we are no longer brothers."

While his brother packed, Emilio stood watch by the door and called him a cab. Estefan was too drunk to drive himself anywhere. Emilio didn't care what happened to him, but he didn't want him hurting someone else.

Estefan protested when Emilio snatched his keys away.

"Call me and tell me where you are, and I'll have your bike delivered to you."

He slurred out a few more threats, then staggered to the cab. Emilio watched it drive away, then he grabbed his case and headed up to his bedroom. Isabelle was sitting on the edge of his bed. She shot to her feet when he stepped in the room.

"He's gone," Emilio said. "And he isn't coming back."

She breathed a sigh of relief.

Emilio dropped his case on the floor by the bed, pulled her into his arms and held her. "I am so sorry. If I even suspected he would pull something like this I never would have let him stay here. And I sure as hell wouldn't have left you alone with him."

"I guess it was a case of unrequited love," she said, her voice still a little wobbly. "Who knew?"

He had, but he never imagined Estefan was capable of rape. He had been raised to respect women. They all had. There was obviously something wrong in Estefan's head.

"When I think what might have happened if I hadn't come home early..." He squeezed her tighter.

"He's going to tell people that I'm staying here, isn't he?"

"You can count on it." Definitely the family. With any luck he wasn't smart enough to go to the press, or they wouldn't listen.

She looked crestfallen. "If I leave today, right now, maybe it won't be so bad. You can deny I was here at all. And I will, too. No one has to know."

She was nearly raped, and she was worried about *him*. It was sickening how he had misjudged her, how he thought she could have anything to do with her husband's crimes. "You're not going anywhere, Izzie."

"But—"

"I don't care if anyone knows you're here."

"Why?"

"Because you're innocent."

"How do you know that?"

He shrugged. "Because I do."

She didn't seem to know what to say.

"There's something we need to talk about, something I need to know."

She frowned, as though she knew she wasn't going to like what was coming next.

"What did your father do when he found out we were eloping?"

"What makes you think he knew?"

"Because Estefan told him."

She sucked in a quiet breath.

"He did it to get back at me. He said he did it to help me, but I know he was just jealous."

"I always wondered how my father found out."

"Is that why he did it?"

"Did what?"

He opened his briefcase, pulled out the file and handed it to her. She started to read the top page and the color leeched from her face. She sank to the edge of the bed.

He sat beside her. "The concussion, the bruised ribs. He did that because of me, didn't he?"

She flipped through the pages, then looked up at him, eyes wide. "Where did you get this?"

"Why didn't you tell me, Izzie? Why didn't you tell me what he did to you?"

She shrugged, setting the file on the bed beside her. "Because that's not the way it works."

"I could have helped you."

She shook her head. "No one could help us."

Us? "Your mother, too?"

"My father was a very angry man. But if there's any justice in this world, I can rest easy knowing he's rotting in hell for what he did to us."

He could barely wrap his head around it. How could he have been so blind? Why didn't he see?

"I know you don't like to talk about it, but I have to know. Why did you do it? Why did you leave me for Betts?"

"It was the only way to keep her safe."

"Your mother?"

She nodded.

"Tell me what happened."

She bit her lip, wringing her hands in her lap.

He took her hand in his and held it. "Please, Isabelle."

"My father found out about us and *punished* me. When he was finished, he told me that if I ever saw you again he was going to disown me. I would be completely cut off. I was so sick of it, I told him I didn't care. I said I didn't want his money, and I didn't care if I ever saw him again.

I said I was going to marry you, and my mother was going to come live with us and nothing he could do would stop me." She took a deep, unsteady breath. "And he said…he said that if I married you, something terrible would happen to my mother. He said she would have an 'accident.'" She looked up at him. "My father did not make idle threats, and the look in his eyes…I knew he would kill her just to spite me. And to prove his point he punished her, too, and it was even worse than what he did to me. She couldn't get out of bed for a week."

Sick bastard. If Isabelle had a concussion and bruised ribs, he couldn't even imagine what he must have put her mother through.

Emilio felt sick to his stomach, sick all the way to his soul. "Did he force you to marry Betts?"

"Not exactly. Usually he was good about hiding the marks, but this time he didn't even try. My parents had been friends with Lenny for years. Long story short, he happened to stop by and saw the condition we were in. He was horrified. He'd suspected that my father was abusive, but he had no idea how bad it was. He wanted to call the police, but my mom begged him not to."

"Why? They could have helped you."

"Because she tried that before. My father was a very powerful man. The charges had a way of disappearing."

Alejandro had said as much.

"Lenny figured if he couldn't help my mother, he could at least get me out of there. He knew my father would agree to a marriage."

"A marriage between his nineteen-year-old daughter and a man in his forties?"

"My father saw it as a business opportunity. He had debts, and Lenny promised to make them go away."

The gambling Alejandro had mentioned. Just when

Emilio didn't think he could feel more disgust, her father sank to a whole new level of vile. "He *sold* you."

She shrugged. "More or less."

"So what was the going rate for a nineteen-year-old virgin?"

She lowered her eyes. "Lenny wouldn't tell me. Hundreds of thousands. Maybe millions. Who knows."

"If you had told me then, I would have taken you away. You and your mother. I would have killed your father if that's what it took to keep you both safe. I would kill him now if he wasn't already dead."

"And that's exactly why I couldn't tell you. If you only knew how many times she tried to leave. But he always found us and brought us back. He would have hurt you if you had tried to help. Look what he did to your mother just to spite me. At least Lenny had been able to take me away from it. And you were safe and free to live your life."

It was hard to fathom that Izzie's husband, a man that Emilio had despised for so many years, had really saved her life.

Only to turn around and ruin it again, he reminded himself.

"The sad fact is, I never should have come to see you that day on campus," Izzie said. "I should have known he would never let it happen, not if there wasn't something in it for him."

"I've never said this about another human being, but I'm glad your father is dead."

Her smile was a sad one. "No more than my mother and I."

"I'm sorry I've been such a jerk."

She shrugged. "I hurt you."

"That doesn't make it right."

She reached up, stroked his cheek. "Emilio, not a day

has gone by when I didn't miss you, and wished it were you I had married. It's going to sound silly, but I never stopped loving you. I still haven't."

A sudden surge of emotion caught him completely by surprise. He slipped his arms around her and pulled her against him, pressed his face against the softness of her hair. He wanted to hold her close and never let go, yet he couldn't help thinking he didn't deserve her love. He'd failed her, and all because he couldn't see past his own wounded pride. He should have trusted her. When he read in the papers that she was marrying Betts, he should have known something was wrong, that she would never willingly betray him.

He had promised to take care of her, to protect her and he'd let her down when she needed him most.

"Isabelle—"

She put her fingers over his lips to shush him. "No more talking."

She slid her arms around his neck and kissed him. And kept kissing him, until the past ceased to matter. All he cared about was being close to her. They would start over today, this very minute, and things would be different this time. He would take care of her and protect her. The way it should have been fifteen years ago.

Though there was no rush, Isabelle seemed in a hurry to get them both naked. She shoved his jacket off his shoulders, then undid the buttons on his shirt and pushed that off, too. Then she unbuttoned her dress and pulled it up over her head. Her bra was next to go, until all that was left was her panties.

She took those off, then pulled back the covers and stretched out on the bed, summoning him with a smile and a crooked finger.

"I like that you're not shy anymore," he said rising to take off his pants.

"There are no bruises or marks to hide now."

He hadn't even considered that. "Is that why you never let me see you undressed?"

"I wanted to, but I knew there would be questions."

"Isabelle."

"No more talking about the past. Let's concentrate on today. On right now. Make love to me, and nothing else will matter."

That was by far the best idea she'd had all day.

Fourteen

Emilio stripped out of his clothes and climbed into bed with Isabelle. Since Tuesday she hadn't stopped thinking about making love to him again. Only this time she wasn't nervous. This time she had nothing to hide. He knew her secrets. She could relax and be herself. Until the weight of everything she had hidden from him was finally gone, she hadn't realized what a heavy load she'd carried. And when Emilio took her in his arms and kissed her, she knew he was back to being the man he used to be. Sweet and tender and thoughtful.

Ironically that wasn't what she wanted now. She was eager to experiment. She wanted it to be crazy and exciting. There were hundreds of different ways to make love and she wanted to try as many as she could before she had to go. She wanted it to be fun.

"Emilio, I'm not going to break."

He gazed down at her, brow furrowed. "I just don't

want to hurt you again. And after what happened to you today…if you want to wait, we can take a few days."

They had so little time left, she didn't want to waste any of it. And she didn't want him to feel as if he had to treat her with kid gloves. "First of all, if you're referring to Tuesday night, you did not hurt me."

Up went the brow.

"Okay, maybe it hurt a little, but only for a minute. And it wasn't a bad hurt, if that makes sense. And after that it was…*amazing.* And as far as what happened today, yeah it scared the hell out of me, but that has nothing to do with us. I know you would never hurt me."

"But I did." He stroked her hair back from her face, touched her cheek. "I've been a total jerk the last couple weeks, and you've done absolutely nothing to deserve it."

"Except the rug, and the casserole dish, and the pink laundry. And of course the scorched shirt."

"That doesn't count. I put you in a position to fail so I could throw it back in your face."

"And I've forgiven you."

He sighed and rolled onto his back. "Maybe that's part of the problem. Maybe I feel like I don't deserve your forgiveness."

She sat up beside him. "In that case, you have to forgive *yourself.* You've got to let it go. Trust me on this one. If I hadn't made peace with my father, and Lenny, I would probably be in a padded room by now."

"How? How do you let it go?"

She shrugged. "You just do."

"I'm just so…*mad.*"

"At yourself?"

"At myself, and at your father. For what he did to you, and everything he stole from us. Everything that we could have been. If it wasn't for him, we would be married, we would probably have kids." He pushed himself up on his elbows. "I'm pissed at Estefan for ratting us out, and Alejandro for prosecuting you when I'm pretty sure he knows damn well that you're innocent. I'm pissed at every person who suspected your father was abusive and did nothing about it. I feel like I'm mad at the whole damned world!"

"So let it out."

"I can't."

"Yes, you can." She reached over and pinched his left nipple. Hard.

"Hey!" He batted her hand away, looking stunned, as if he couldn't believe she would do something like that. Sweet, nonconfrontational Isabelle. "What was that for?"

He was going to have to accept that she had changed. "Did it hurt?"

"Yeah, it hurt."

"Good." She did the same thing to the right side.

"Ow! Stop that!"

She pinched the fleshy skin under his bicep next and he jerked away.

"Izzie, stop it."

She climbed into his lap, straddling his thighs. "Make me."

She moved to pinch him again and his hand shot out to manacle her wrist, and when she tried to use her other hand, he grabbed that wrist, too. She struggled to yank free, but he held on tighter, almost to the point of pain. But that was good, that was what she wanted. She didn't want him to look at her as some frail flower he needed to protect. She wanted him to know how tough she was.

Since her hands were restrained, she leaned in and bit him instead, on his left shoulder. Not hard enough to break the skin, but enough to cause pain.

He jerked away. "Isabelle! What's gotten into you?"

"Are you pissed?"

"Yes, I'm pissed!"

"Good." She leaned in to do it again, but he'd apparently had enough. Finally. He pulled her down on top of him then rolled her onto her back, pinning her wrists over her head.

She'd never thought of herself as the type who would be into anything even remotely kinky, but she was so hot for him, she was afraid she might spontaneously combust. Emilio settled between her thighs, holding her to the mattress with the weight of his body, and it was clear that he liked it, too. A lot.

She hooked her legs around his, arching against him. He groaned and his eyes went dark, breath rasped out. So she did it again, bucking against him.

"Izzie." His voice held a warning, stop or else, but she *wanted* the "or else."

Lifting her head, she scraped her teeth across his nipple. She would keep biting and pinching and bucking until he gave her what she wanted. Only this time he turned the tables on her. He dipped his head and took her nipple in his mouth, sucked hard.

She cried out, pushing against his hands, digging her nails into her palms. *"Yesss."*

"You *like* this," he said.

His eyes said that he'd finally figured it out. He knew what she wanted.

It was about damned time.

She knew Emilio liked to be composed at all times, but she wanted him to lose control, to do something crazy.

He kissed her, like he never had before. A hard, punishing kiss. He started to work his way down, to her neck and her shoulders, kissing and nipping. Then he slipped lower still, letting go of her wrists so he could press her thighs wide. She thought they would make love right away, but clearly he had other ideas.

She held her breath in anticipation, gasping as he took her in his mouth. Oral sex had been a regular routine for them, and it was always good, but never like this. He was *devouring* her. She clawed her nails through his hair, so close to losing it…then he thrust a finger inside of her, then another, then a third, slow and deep, and pleasure seized her like a wild animal.

Emilio rose up and settled between her thighs, thrusting hard inside of her, and the orgasm that had begun to ebb slowly away suddenly picked up momentum again, only this time from somewhere deep inside. Somewhere she'd never felt before. Maybe her soul. It erupted into a sensation so beautiful and perfect, so exactly what she ever hoped it could be, tears welled in her eyes. And she was so utterly lost in her own pleasure she didn't realize he had come, too, until he flopped onto his back beside her.

"Wow," he said, breathing hard.

"So, are you still mad?"

He laughed—a genuine honest to goodness laugh. A sound she hadn't heard out of him in a very long time. "Not at all. In fact, I can't recall the last time I was so relaxed."

She smiled and curled up against his side. "Good."

"I didn't hurt you?"

"Are you kidding? That was *perfect.*" And it must have been really good for him, too, because he was still mostly hard. Then she realized something that made her heart drop. "Emilio, you didn't use a condom."

"I know."

She shot up in bed. "You *know?* You did it *deliberately?*"

He didn't even have the decency to look remorseful.

"Not exactly. I realized the minute I was inside of you, but I didn't think you would appreciate me stopping to roll one on."

"Did it occur to you that I could get pregnant?"

"Of course."

"What did you think? That me being pregnant with his brother's baby will stop Alejandro from putting me in prison? They put pregnant women in prison all the time. Are you prepared to raise a baby alone? To be a single dad for the next twenty-to-life? Maybe if I get out early on good behavior I'll see him graduate high school."

"You're not going to prison."

She groaned and dropped her head in her hands. The man was impossible.

"Do you think you could be pregnant?" he asked.

"My period is due soon, so I'd say it's unlikely."

He actually looked disappointed. How had he gone from hating her one day, to wanting to have babies with her the next? This was crazy. Even if she didn't go to prison his family would never accept her.

"Can I ask you a question?" he said.

"Sure."

"Since you've told me everything else, would you explain how you never slept with Lenny? Because I really don't get it. I can't go five minutes without wanting to rip your clothes off."

"He had a heart condition and he was impotent. Ultimately he did screw me, just not in the bedroom."

"After your father died you could have divorced him."

"There didn't seem to be much point. There was only one other man I wanted." She touched his arm. "And I knew he would never take me back, never forgive me."

"I guess you were wrong."

"It would probably be better if you hadn't."

"You're *not* going to prison."

"Yes, I am. Nothing is going to stop that now."

"I just got you back, Izzie. I'm not letting you go again."

But he was going to have to. He couldn't keep her out of prison by sheer will. He was going to have to accept that they were living on borrowed time.

"Things are going to change around here," he said.

"What things?"

"First off, I'm calling my housekeeper back."

"You can't do that. You gave her the month off. It's not fair."

"So I'll hire a temp."

"But I like doing it."

He raised a brow at her.

"I do. And it gives me something to do. A way to pass the time, since I doubt all those charities I used to volunteer for would be interested in my services any longer."

"Are you sure?"

"Positive."

"Okay, but you're not allowed to wear the uniform anymore. And I'm buying you some decent clothes."

"There's no point."

"There sure as hell is. The ones you have are awful."

"And I'll only need them for another few weeks. Getting anything new would be a waste of money."

She could tell he wanted to argue, but he probably figured there was no point. She was not going to budge on this one. Besides, the last thing she wanted was for him to spend money on her. She didn't deserve it.

"You're obviously not staying in the maid's quarters any longer. You're moving in here with me. If you want to."

"Of course I do." It was probably a bad idea. The closer they got, the harder it would be when she had to go, but she had the feeling nothing would prevent that now. They might as well spend all the time they could together.

"You have a say in this, too," he said. "Is there anything you'd like to add? Anything you want?"

There were so many things she wanted. She wanted to marry him, and have babies with him. She wanted to do everything they had talked about before. It's all she had ever wanted. But why dwell on a future that wasn't meant to be?

The phone rang, so she grabbed the cordless off the bedside table and handed it to him. He looked at the display and cursed under his breath. "Well, that didn't take long."

He sat up and hit the talk button. "Hello, Mama."

Isabelle winced. Estefan hadn't wasted any time running to his mother, had he?

He listened for a minute, then said, "Yes, it's true."

She could hear his mother talking. Not what she was saying, but her tone came through perfectly. She was upset.

"I know he was drunk. Are you really surprised?"

More talking from his mother's end, then Emilio interrupted her. "Why don't I come over there right now so we can talk about this?"

She must have agreed, because then he said, "I'll be over as soon as I can."

He hung up and set the phone back on the table. "I guess you got the gist of that."

"Yeah."

"I shouldn't be too long."

"Take your time." He wasn't the only one who needed to talk to their mother. "I was thinking maybe I could go talk to my mother, too. I'd hate for her to hear it from someone besides me."

"I think that's a good idea. I'll pick up Chinese food on my way home."

"Sounds good." Although after dealing with their parents, she wondered if either of them would have much of an appetite.

Fifteen

Emilio parked in the driveway of his mother's condo. The year he'd made his first million he'd bought it for her. He'd wanted to get her something bigger and in a more affluent part of the city, but she had wanted to live here, in what was a primarily Hispanic neighborhood. Not that this place was what anyone would consider shabby. It had been brand-new when he bought it, and he made sure it had every upgrade they offered, and a few he requested special. After sacrificing so much for Emilio and his brothers, she deserved the best of everything.

He walked to the front door and let himself inside. "Mama?"

"In the kitchen," she called back.

He wasn't surprised to find her at the counter, apron on, adding ingredients to a mixing bowl. She always baked when she was upset or angry.

"What are you making?"

"Churros, with extra cinnamon, just the way you like them." She gestured to the kitchen table. "Sit down, I'll get you something to drink."

She pulled a pitcher of iced tea from the fridge and poured him a glass. He would have preferred something stronger, but she never kept alcohol of any kind in the house.

Handing it to him, she went back to the bowl, mixing the contents with a wooden spoon. "I guess you saw your brother's face."

"I saw it."

"He said she attacked him. For no good reason."

"Attempted rape is a pretty good reason."

She cut her eyes to him. "Emilio! Your brother would never do that. He was raised to respect women."

Emphatically as she denied it, something in her eyes said she was afraid it might be true.

"If you had seen Isabelle, the ripped uniform and the bruises on her arms… She was terrified."

She muttered something in Spanish and crossed herself.

"He needs help, Mama."

"I know. He told me that bad people are after him. He asked to stay here. I told him no."

"Good. We can't keep trying to save him. We have to let him hit rock bottom. He has to want to help himself."

"You told him you're no longer brothers. You didn't mean it."

"I did mean it. He hurt the woman I love."

"How can you love her after what she did to you? She left you for that rich man. She only cared about money. That's the only reason she's back now."

"She came to me because she wanted help for her mother, not herself. And she didn't marry Betts for his money. The only reason she left me for him is because her father threatened to hurt her mother."

He waited for the shock, but there was none, confirming what he already suspected. "You knew about the abuse, didn't you? You knew that Isabelle's father was hurting them. You *had* to."

She didn't answer him.

"Mama."

"Of course I knew," she said softly. "The things that man did to them." She closed her eyes and shook her head, as if she were trying to block the mental image. "It made me sick. And poor Mrs. Winthrop. Sometimes he beat her so badly, she would be in bed for days. And Isabelle, she always stayed right by her mother's side. I never speak ill of the dead, but that man did the world a favor when he died."

"You should have told me. I could have helped her."

She shook her head. "No. He would have hurt you, too. I was always afraid that something bad would happen if he found out about you and Isabelle."

"Well, he found out." He almost told her that Estefan was the one who ratted him out, but he didn't want to hurt her any more than necessary.

"You had the potential to go so far, Emilio. I was relieved when she left you."

"Even though you knew how much I loved her?"

"I figured you would get over her eventually."

"But I didn't. As bitter as I was, I never stopped loving her."

Was that guilt in her eyes? "What difference does it make now? Alejandro said she's going to prison."

"Not if I can help it."

She set the spoon down and pushed the bowl aside. "She stole money."

"No, she didn't. She's innocent."

"You know that for a fact?"

"I know it in my heart. In every fiber of my being. She's not a thief."

"Even if that's true, everyone thinks she's guilty."

He shrugged. "I don't care what everyone thinks."

"Emilio—"

"Mama, do you remember what you told me when I asked you why you never remarried? You said Papa was your one true love, and there could be no one else. I finally understand what you meant. I was lucky enough to get Izzie back. I can't lose her again."

"Even if it means ruining everything you've worked so hard for?"

"That's not going to happen. First thing Monday, I'm hiring a new attorney."

"People will find out."

"They probably will."

"And I could argue with you until I'm blue in the face and it won't do any good, will it?"

He shook his head.

She drew in a deep breath, then blew it out. "Then I will pray for you, Emilio. For you and Isabelle."

"Thank you, Mama." At this point, he would take all the help he could get.

Isabelle called her mother Friday, but she was out with Ben. They went to dinner with friends, then they left Saturday morning for an overnight trip to Phoenix to see an old college buddy of Ben's. Isabelle didn't get a chance to talk to her until Monday morning. She took the news much better than Isabelle expected. In fact, she suspected all along that Isabelle had been "bending" the truth.

"Sweetheart," she said, fixing them each a cup of tea

in her tiny kitchenette. "You know I can always tell when you're lying. And, *Mrs. Smith?*"

Isabelle couldn't help but smile. "Not very creative, huh?"

"I thought it was awfully coincidental that you were working in the same neighborhood where Emilio lived. Then I mentioned him and you got very nervous."

"And people think I'm capable of stealing millions of dollars." She sighed. "Not only am I a terrible liar, but I don't even know how to balance a checkbook."

Her mother walked over with their tea and sat down at the table.

"I'm sorry I lied to you, but I promised Emilio I wouldn't tell anyone I was staying there. It was part of our deal."

"Emilio is going to help you, right?"

"He's going to talk to his brother on your behalf. You won't be serving any time."

"But what about you?"

They had been through this so many times. "There isn't anything he can do. You know what Lenny's lawyer said. The evidence against me is indisputable."

"There has to be something Emilio can do. Can't he talk to his brother? Make some sort of deal?"

She was just as bad as Emilio, refusing to accept reality. She wished they would both stop being so stubborn. But she didn't want her mother to worry so she said, "I'll ask him, okay?"

Her mother looked relieved.

"So, tell me about this weekend trip. Did you have fun?"

She lit up like a firefly. "We had a *wonderful* time. Ben has the nicest friends. The only thing that was a little unexpected was that they put us in a bedroom together."

Her brows rose. "Oh really?"

"Nothing happened," she said, then her cheeks turned

red and she added, "Well, nothing much. But he is a very nice kisser."

"Only nice?"

Her smile was shy, with a touch of mischief. "Okay, better than nice."

They talked about her trip with Ben and what they had planned for the coming weekend. He clearly adored her mother, and the feeling was mutual. Isabelle was so happy she had found someone who appreciated her, and made her feel good about herself. At the same time she was a little sad that she wouldn't be around to see their relationship grow. Of course, they could always write letters, and her mother could visit.

Maybe she was a little jealous, too, that she had finally found her heart's desire, and it had to end in only a few weeks. They wouldn't even get to spend Christmas together.

She drove back to Emilio's fighting the urge to feel sorry for herself. When she pulled in the driveway there was an unfamiliar car parked there. A silver Lexus. She considered pulling back out. What if it was someone who shouldn't know she was staying there? But hadn't Emilio said he didn't care who knew?

She pulled the Saab in the garage and let herself in the house. Emilio met her at the door. "There you are. I was about send out a search party."

"I went to see my mother."

"Is everything okay? She wasn't angry?"

"Not at all."

"I need to get you a cell phone, so I can reach you when you're out."

For less than a month? What was the point? "Is there something wrong?"

"Nothing. In fact, I have some good news. Come in the living room, there's someone I want you to meet."

There was a man sitting on the couch, a slew of papers on the table in front of him. When they entered the room, he stood.

"Isabelle, this is David Morrison."

He was around Emilio's age, very attractive and dressed in a sharp, tailored suit. "Ms. Winthrop," he said, shaking her hand. "It's a pleasure to meet you."

"You, too," she said, shooting Emilio a questioning look.

"David is a defense attorney. One of the best. He's going to be taking over your case."

"What?"

"We're firing Clifton Stone."

"But…why?"

"Because he's giving you bad advice," Mr. Morrison said. "I've been going over your case. The evidence against you is flimsy at best. We'll take this to trial if necessary, but honestly, I don't think it will come down to that."

"I was using Lenny's lawyer because he was representing me pro bono. I can't afford a lawyer."

"It's taken care of," Emilio said.

She shook her head. "I can't let you do this."

"The retainer is paid. Nonrefundable. It's done."

"But I can't go to trial. The only way my mother will avoid prison is if I plead out." She turned to her "new" attorney. "Mr. Morrison—"

"Please, call me David."

"David, I really appreciate you coming to see me, but I can't do this."

"Ms. Winthrop, do you want to spend the next twenty years in prison?"

Was this a trick question? Did anyone *want* to go to prison? "Of course not."

"If you stick with your current attorney, that's what will happen. I've seen lawyers reprimanded and in some cases disbarred for giving such blatantly negligent counsel. Either he's completely incompetent, or he has some sort of agenda."

Agenda? How could he possibly benefit from her going to prison? "What about my mother? What happens to her?"

"Alejandro already told me they wouldn't ask for more than probation," Emilio said.

"When did he say that?"

He hesitated, then said, "The day you came to see me in my office."

So all this time she'd been working for him for no reason? She should be furious, but the truth was, it was a million times better here than at that dumpy motel. And if she hadn't come here, Emilio would have gone the rest of his life hating her. Maybe now they even had some sort of future together. Marriage and family, just like they had planned. Hope welled up with such intensity she had to fight it back down. She was afraid to believe it was real.

"You really think you could keep me and my mother out of prison?" she asked David.

"Worst case you may end up with probation. It would go a long way if the last few million of the missing money were to surface."

"If I knew where it was I would have handed it over months ago. I gave them everything else."

"I'm going to do some digging and see what turns up. In the meantime, I need you to sign a notice of change of counsel to make it official."

She signed the document, but only after thoroughly reading it—she had learned her lesson with Lenny—then David packed up his things and left.

"I told you I wouldn't let you go to prison," Emilio said,

sounding smug, fixing himself a sandwich before he went back to work.

"I still don't like that you're paying for it. What if someone finds out?"

"I've already said a dozen times—"

"You don't care who finds out. I know. But I do. Until I know for sure that I'm not going to prison, I don't want anyone to know. Even if that means waiting through a trial."

"I suppose that means we'll have to wait to get married."

Married? She opened her mouth to speak, but nothing came out. She knew he wanted to be with her, but this was the first time he had actually mentioned marriage.

"I was hoping we could start a family right away," he said, putting the turkey and the mayo back in the fridge. "If we haven't already, that is. But we've waited this long. I guess a few more months won't kill me. Just so long as you know that I love you, and no matter what happens, I'm not letting you go again."

He loved her, and wanted to marry her, and have a family with her. She threw her arms around him and hugged him tight. This was more than she ever could have hoped for. "I love you, too, Emilio."

"This is all going to work out," he told her, and she was actually starting to believe it.

"So, do you have to go back to work?" she asked, sliding her hands under his jacket and up his chest.

He grinned down at her. "That depends what you have in mind."

Though they had spent the better part of the weekend making love in bed—and on the bedroom floor and in the shower, and even on the dining room table—she could never get enough of him. "We haven't done it in the kitchen yet."

He lifted her up and set her on the counter, sliding her skirt up her thighs. "Well, that's an oversight we need to take care of immediately."

Sixteen

Isabelle never imagined things could be so wonderful. She and Emilio were going to get married and have a family—even though he hadn't officially asked her yet—and she and her mother weren't going to prison. Her life was as close to perfect as it could be, yet she had this gut feeling that the other shoe was about to drop. That things were a little *too* perfect.

Emilio wasn't helping matters.

He called her from work Thursday morning to warn her that a package would be arriving. But it wasn't one package. It was a couple dozen, all filled with clothes and shoes from department stores and boutiques all over town. It was an entire wardrobe, and it was exactly what she would have picked for herself.

Her first instinct was tell him to send it back, but now that she wasn't going to prison she did need new clothes.

"How did you know what I would like?" she asked Emilio when she called to thank him.

"I had help."

"What kind of help?"

"A personal shopper, so to speak. I swore her to secrecy."

Her? Who would know her exact taste, that Emilio knew to contact? There was really only one person. "My *mother?*"

"I knew you wouldn't get the clothes yourself, and who better to know what you like?"

"I talked to her this morning and she didn't say a word."

"She wanted it to be a surprise. If there's anything that you don't like just put it aside and I'll have it returned."

"It's all perfect."

"There should be something coming later this afternoon, too. A few things I picked out."

Isabelle called her mother to thank her, but she wasn't home so she left a message. After that she waited, very impatiently, until the package with Emilio's purchases arrived later that afternoon. She carried it into the living room where she had been sorting and folding all the other things.

Sitting on the couch, she ripped it open. It was lingerie. The first two items she pulled out were soft silk gowns in pink and white. When she saw what was underneath the gowns she actually blushed. Sexy items of silk and lace that were scandalously revealing. She'd never owned anything so provocative. There had never been any point.

She called Emilio immediately to thank him.

"I wasn't sure if they would be a little too racy," he said.

"No, I love them!"

"You'll have to try them on for me later."

"I might just be wearing one when you walk in the door," she said, and could practically feel his sexy smile right through the phone line.

"In that case I may just have to come home early."

After they hung up Isabelle was gathering all her new clothes to take upstairs when the doorbell rang again.

More new clothes?

She walked to the foyer and pulled the door open, expecting another delivery man, but when she saw who was standing there her heart plummeted. "Mrs. Suarez."

"May I come in?" Emilio's mother asked.

"Of course," she said, stepping aside so she could come inside. "Emilio isn't here."

"I came to talk to you."

The last time she had seen Mrs. Suarez, Isabelle's father had been accusing her of stealing from them. And after threatening to have her arrested, and her younger children taken away by Social Services, he'd fired her.

The phone started to ring. "Let me grab that really fast," Isabelle said, dashing to the living room where she'd left the cordless phone, answering with a breathless, "Hello?"

It was her mother. "Hi honey, I just got your message. I'm so glad you like the clothes. Wasn't that a sweet thing for Emilio to do?"

"Yes, it was. Mom, can I call you back?"

"Is everything okay?"

"Everything is fine." She glanced over and realized Mrs. Suarez had followed her. She was looking at the piles of clothes strewn over the furniture, specifically the lingerie, and she did not look happy.

Oh, hell.

"I'll call you soon." She disconnected and turned to Mrs. Suarez. "Sorry about that."

"How is your mother?"

"Really good." She gestured to the one chair that wasn't piled with clothes. "Please, sit down. Can I get you something to drink?"

His mother sat. "No, thank you."

Isabelle moved some of the clothes from the end of the couch and sat down.

"It looks like you've been shopping." With her son's money her look said. Talk about awkward.

"Actually, Emilio had my mother pick them out and they were delivered a little while ago."

"He's a very generous man." Her tone suggested that generosity was wasted on someone like Isabelle. Or maybe Isabelle was being paranoid. Put in his mother's position, she might not trust her, either.

There was an awkward pause, and Isabelle blurted out, "I'm so sorry for what happened with Estefan."

She looked puzzled. "Why are *you* sorry? Emilio said Estefan forced himself on you. You had every right to defend yourself. I see the bruises are fading."

Isabelle glanced down at her arms. The marks Estefan had left there had faded to a greenish-yellow. "I still feel bad for scratching him."

"Estefan is part of the reason I'm here. I wanted to apologize on his behalf. I felt it was my duty as his mother."

"Is he okay?"

"I don't know. He disappeared again. It could be months before I see him." Isabelle must have looked guilty because Mrs. Suarez added, "This is not your fault."

Logically she knew that, but she felt responsible.

"I also wanted to talk to you about Emilio."

She'd assumed as much.

"He says you're innocent."

"I have a new attorney. He says he thinks I'll be acquitted, or let off with probation."

"And Emilio is paying for this new lawyer?"

"I didn't want him to, but he insisted. And if he hadn't, I would have spent the next twenty years in prison."

"Emilio has done you many favors. Now I want you to do him a favor."

"Of course. Anything."

"Leave."

Leave? She didn't know what to say.

"Only until you are found innocent." Her eyes pleaded with Isabelle. "My son has worked so hard to get where he is, and because he loves you, he would risk throwing it all away. If you love him, you won't allow that to happen."

"And if I'm not acquitted? If I wind up with probation?"

Mrs. Suarez didn't say anything, but it was written all over her face. She wanted Isabelle to leave him for good. And her reasoning was totally logical.

The CFO of a company like Western Oil couldn't be married to a woman out on probation for financial fraud. They would have no choice but to fire him, and he would never find another job like it. At least, not one that would pay him even a fraction of what he was worth. Not to mention that he would lose all his friends.

Because of her, he would be a pariah.

He said he loved her and didn't care what people thought, but with his life in shambles he might feel differently. He would begin to resent her, and they would be right back to where they were before, only this time he would hate her not for leaving, but for staying. She couldn't do that to him.

Just once she had wanted something for herself, she

had wanted to be happy. For the first time in her life she wanted to do something selfish.

But Mrs. Suarez was right. It was time for her to go.

"I had an interesting talk with Cassandra," Adam said from Emilio's office doorway.

He glanced up from his computer screen. He had just a few things he needed to finish up before he went home for the night. "Is there another public relations nightmare on the horizon?"

"You tell me."

"Meaning what?"

He stepped into his office and shut the door. "Cassandra got a call from a reporter asking if it was true that there was a connection between Isabelle Winthrop-Betts and the CFO of Western Oil."

He sighed. *Here we go.*

"What did she tell them?"

"That she knows of no association, then she came and asked me about it. So I'm asking you, what's the status of her case? Someone is digging, and I get the feeling something big is about to break."

"I hired a new attorney. He wants to take it to trial. He thinks he can get an acquittal."

"But it will take some time."

"Probably."

Adam shook his head.

"If you have something to say, just say it, Adam."

"If she goes to trial and the story breaks about the two of you... Emilio, the damage will be done. You'll never make CEO. The board would never allow it. I can't guarantee they won't vote to terminate you immediately."

"Let me ask you something. Suppose Katy was accused

of a crime, and you knew she was innocent. Would you stand behind her, even if it meant making sacrifices?"

Adam took a deep breath and blew it out. "Yes, of course I would."

"Then why is everyone so surprised that I'm standing behind Isabelle? Do I want to be CEO? Do I think I'm the best man for the job? You're damn right I do. But what kind of CEO, what kind of *man* would I be if didn't stand up for the things I believe in? If I abandoned Isabelle when she needs me most?"

"You're right," Adam said. "I admire what you're doing, and I'll back you as long as I can."

"I know you will. And when it comes to the point that you can't help me, don't lose a night's sleep over it. This is my choice."

His secretary buzzed him. "I'm sorry to interrupt, Mr. Suarez, but your brother is on line one. He says it's important."

"Which brother?"

"Alejandro."

"Go ahead and take it," Adam said. "We'll talk later."

Adam left, and Emilio hit the button for line one. "Hey, Alejandro, what's up?"

"Hey, big brother, I was wondering if you're going to be home this evening."

"This was so important you would interrupt a meeting with my boss?"

"Actually, it is. I need to talk to you. In person."

"What time?"

"The earlier the better. Alana doesn't like it when I come home too late."

Emilio thought about Isabelle's promise to model the new lingerie. If he met with Alejandro early, then he and Isabelle would have the rest of the evening.

"Why don't you meet me at my house in an hour?"

"Sounds good. Will Isabelle be there?"

"Of course. Is that a problem?"

"No, I'll see you in an hour."

Seventeen

As his driver took him home, Emilio got to thinking about what Alejandro could possibly need to discuss that was so urgent. It couldn't have anything to do with Isabelle's case, because he wasn't allowed to question her without her lawyer present.

His driver dropped him at the front door and Emilio let himself inside—and nearly tripped over the suitcases sitting there. "What the hell?"

Isabelle appeared at the top of the stairs, and she was clearly surprised to see him. She was dressed in what he was guessing were her new clothes. She looked young and hip and classy. So different from the scrawny, desperate woman who had come to see him in his office.

"You're home early," she said, her tone suggesting that wasn't a good thing.

"Yeah, I'm home." He set his briefcase on the floor next to the open door. "What the hell is going on?"

She walked down the stairs, met him in foyer. "I was going to leave you a note."

"You're going somewhere?"

"I'm moving out."

"Why?"

"Because I have to. I can't let you risk your career for me."

"Isabelle—"

"I'm not talking forever. As soon as I'm acquitted we can be together again. But until then, we can't see each other. Not at all. If your career was ruined because of me, your family would never forgive me, and I would never forgive myself."

"And what if you aren't acquitted? David said you might possibly get probation."

She bit her lip, and he could guess the answer.

"I'm not losing you again, Isabelle."

"Hopefully you won't have to. I'm going to fight it Emilio. I will do anything I have to for an acquittal. But if I don't get it…I'm not sure how, but I'll pay you back for the lawyer's fee."

"I don't give a damn about the lawyer's fees. And I'm not letting you do this."

"You don't have a choice."

He could see by her expression that she meant it. She was really leaving, whether he liked it or not. His heart started to race and suddenly he couldn't pull in enough air. The thought of losing her again filled him with a sense of panic that seemed to well up from the center of his being.

This could not be happening. Not again.

"Knock, knock," someone said, and they both turned to see Alejandro standing on the porch at the open door. He stepped inside, saw the suitcases and asked Isabelle, "Going somewhere?"

"Nowhere out of your jurisdiction, if that's what you're worried about. I'm going to stay at my mother's for a while."

"No, she isn't," Emilio said.

She cut her eyes to him. "*Yes,* I am."

"Can I ask why?" Alejandro said.

"She's worried that her being here is going to damage my career, despite the fact that I keep telling her I don't give a *damn* about my career."

"I think you both need to listen to what I have to say."

"If has to do with my case, I can't talk to you without my lawyer present," Isabelle said.

"Trust me, you're going to want to hear this."

"I won't answer any questions."

"You won't have to." He handed her a white 6x9 envelope Emilio hadn't even noticed he was holding. "Open it."

She did and dropped the contents into her hand, looking confused. "My passport?"

"I don't get it," Emilio said. "Are you suggesting she should leave the country?"

Alejandro laughed. "I thought she might like it back, now that all the charges against her have been formally dropped."

Emilio was certain he misheard him. "Say again?"

"All the charges against Isabelle have been dropped."

Emilio looked over at Isabelle and realized she was practically hyperventilating.

"And my mother?" she asked.

"Your mother, too."

"You're serious?" she said. "This isn't just some twisted joke?"

"It's no joke."

She pressed her hand over her heart and tears welled in her eyes. She turned to Emilio. "Oh, my God, it's over."

He held out his arms and she walked into them, hugging him hard, saying, "I can't believe it's really over."

"What the hell happened?" Emilio asked his brother.

Isabelle turned in his arms and said, "Yeah, what the hell happened?"

Alejandro grinned. "You want the full story, or the condensed version?"

"Maybe we should go for the condensed version," she said. "Since you'll have to explain it all to me again when my head stops spinning."

"It was your husband's lawyer, Clifton Stone. He had the missing money."

"Stone?" Isabelle said, looking genuinely shocked. "I had no idea he was involved. I never even considered it."

"Is that why he wanted her to take a plea?" Emilio asked. "To take the attention off himself?"

"Yeah. Dumb move on his part. It's what made us suspicious in the first place, but we knew he wouldn't cooperate. We had to flush him out. We figured if we were patient he would do something stupid."

"So you knew all along that she was innocent?" Emilio asked.

"If I thought she was guilty do you think I would have dropped you all those bread crumbs, Emilio? I wanted you to get curious, to take matters into your own hands. And it worked. When you hired the new defense attorney, Stone panicked. He was going to run, and he led us right to the money."

"And he told you I wasn't involved?" Isabelle asked.

"He must have been paranoid about being caught because he saved every piece of correspondence between himself and your husband. Phone calls, emails, texts, you name it. He offered them up in exchange for a plea. He said they would exonerate you and your mother."

"And they did?" Emilio asked.

"Oh yeah. They were full of interesting information. If Betts hadn't died, I'm sure Stone would have flipped on him to save his own neck."

"So that's it?" Isabelle asked. "It's done?"

"The case is officially closed."

Emilio shook his brother's hand. "Thank you, Alejandro."

"Yes, thank you," Isabelle said.

"Well, I'm going to get out of here. I get the feeling you two have a lot to talk about." He started out the door, then stopped and turned back. "How about dinner at my place this weekend? Just the four of us. And the kids, of course."

That was an olive branch if Emilio had ever seen one.

"I'd like that," Isabelle said.

"Great. I'll have Alana call you and you can figure out a time." He shot his brother one last grin then left, shutting the door behind him.

Isabelle turned to Emilio and wrapped her arms around him. "I still can't believe it's really over. It feels like a dream."

"Does this mean you'll stay now?"

She looked up at him. "Only if you want me to."

He laughed. "You think? I had only reduced myself to *begging*."

She smiled up at him. "Then yes, I'll stay."

"We need to celebrate. We should open some champagne."

"Definitely."

"Or we could go out and celebrate."

She rose up on her toes to kiss him. "I think I'd rather

stay in tonight. I seem to recall a promise to model some lingerie."

A smile spread across his face. "I think I like the sound of that. But there's something I need to do first. Something I should have done a long time ago."

"What?"

He had hoped to do this in a more romantic setting, but he couldn't imagine a better time than now. "Isabelle, I never thought we would get a second chance together, and I don't want to spend another day without knowing that you'll be mine forever." He dropped down on one knee and took her hand. "Would you marry me?"

Tears welled in her eyes. "Of course I'll marry you."

He rose and pulled the ring box from his jacket pocket. "This is for you."

She opened it, and her look of surprise, followed by genuine confusion, was understandable.

"At this point you're wondering why a man of my means would give you a 1/4 carat diamond ring of questionable quality."

She was too polite to say he was right, but he could see it in her face.

"When I asked you to marry me before, I couldn't afford a ring, and you couldn't wear one anyway, because your father would find out. We decided that we would look for one together the day before we eloped. Remember?"

"I remember."

"Well, I couldn't wait. I saved up for months and bought this for you."

"And you kept it all this time?"

He shrugged. "I just couldn't let it go. I guess maybe deep down I hoped we'd get a second chance. I know it's small, and if you don't want to wear it I completely understand. I thought you might want to turn it into a necklace, or—"

"No." She took the ring from him, tears rolling down her cheeks, and slipped it on her finger. "You could offer me the Hope Diamond and it would never come close to meaning as much to me as this does."

"Are you sure?"

"Absolutely. I'll wear it forever."

He touched her cheek. "I love you, Isabelle."

"I love you so much." She rose up on her toes and kissed him, then she touched his face, as if she couldn't believe it was real. "Is this really happening?"

"Why do you sound so surprised?"

"Because I always thought I wasn't supposed to be this happy, that it just wasn't in the cards for me. That for some reason I didn't deserve it. And suddenly I've got everything I ever hoped for. I keep thinking it has to be a dream."

"It's very real, and you do deserve it." And he planned to spend the rest of his life proving it to her.

* * * * *

COMING NEXT MONTH

Available August 9, 2011

#2101 MARRIAGE AT THE COWBOY'S COMMAND
Ann Major

#2102 THE REBEL TYCOON RETURNS
Katherine Garbera
Texas Cattleman's Club: The Showdown

#2103 TO TOUCH A SHEIKH
Olivia Gates
Pride of Zohayd

#2104 HOW TO SEDUCE A BILLIONAIRE
Kate Carlisle

#2105 CLAIMING HIS ROYAL HEIR
Jennifer Lewis
Billionaires and Babies

#2106 A CLANDESTINE CORPORATE AFFAIR
Michelle Celmer
Black Gold Billionaires

You can find more information on upcoming
Harlequin® titles, free excerpts and more at
www.HarlequinInsideRomance.com.

HDCNM0711

REQUEST YOUR FREE BOOKS!

2 FREE NOVELS PLUS 2 FREE GIFTS!

Harlequin

Desire

ALWAYS POWERFUL, PASSIONATE AND PROVOCATIVE

YES! Please send me 2 FREE Harlequin Desire® novels and my 2 FREE gifts (gifts are worth about $10). After receiving them, if I don't wish to receive any more books, I can return the shipping statement marked "cancel." If I don't cancel, I will receive 6 brand-new novels every month and be billed just $4.30 per book in the U.S. or $4.99 per book in Canada. That's a saving of at least 14% off the cover price! It's quite a bargain! Shipping and handling is just 50¢ per book in the U.S. and 75¢ per book in Canada.* I understand that accepting the 2 free books and gifts places me under no obligation to buy anything. I can always return a shipment and cancel at any time. Even if I never buy another book, the two free books and gifts are mine to keep forever.

225/326 HDN FEF3

Name   (PLEASE PRINT)

Address   Apt. #

City   State/Prov.   Zip/Postal Code

Signature (if under 18, a parent or guardian must sign)

Mail to the **Reader Service:**
IN U.S.A.: P.O. Box 1867, Buffalo, NY 14240-1867
IN CANADA: P.O. Box 609, Fort Erie, Ontario L2A 5X3

Not valid for current subscribers to Harlequin Desire books.

Want to try two free books from another line?
Call 1-800-873-8635 or visit www.ReaderService.com.

* Terms and prices subject to change without notice. Prices do not include applicable taxes. Sales tax applicable in N.Y. Canadian residents will be charged applicable taxes. Offer not valid in Quebec. This offer is limited to one order per household. All orders subject to credit approval. Credit or debit balances in a customer's account(s) may be offset by any other outstanding balance owed by or to the customer. Please allow 4 to 6 weeks for delivery. Offer available while quantities last.

Your Privacy—The Reader Service is committed to protecting your privacy. Our Privacy Policy is available online at www.ReaderService.com or upon request from the Reader Service.

We make a portion of our mailing list available to reputable third parties that offer products we believe may interest you. If you prefer that we not exchange your name with third parties, or if you wish to clarify or modify your communication preferences, please visit us at www.ReaderService.com/consumerchoice or write to us at Reader Service Preference Service, P.O. Box 9062, Buffalo, NY 14269. Include your complete name and address.

HDES11B

*Once bitten, twice shy. That's Gabby Wade's motto—
especially when it comes to Adamson men.
And the moment she meets Jon Adamson her theory
is confirmed. But with each encounter a little something
sparks between them, making her wonder if she's been
too hasty to dismiss this one!*

*Enjoy this sneak peek from ONE GOOD REASON
by Sarah Mayberry, available August 2011
from Harlequin® Superromance®.*

Gabby Wade's heartbeat thumped in her ears as she marched to her office. She wanted to pretend it was because of her brisk pace returning from the file room, but she wasn't that good a liar.

Her heart was beating like a tom-tom because Jon Adamson had touched her. In a very male, very possessive way. She could still feel the heat of his big hand burning through the seat of her khakis as he'd steadied her on the ladder.

It had taken every ounce of self-control to tell him to unhand her. What she'd really wanted was to grab him by his shirt and, well, explore all those urges his touch had instantly brought to life.

While she might not like him, she was wise enough to understand that it wasn't always about liking the other person. Sometimes it was about pure animal attraction.

Refusing to think about it, she turned to work. When she'd typed in the wrong figures three times, Gabby admitted she was too tired and too distracted. Time to call it a day.

As she was leaving, she spied Jon at his workbench in the shop. His head was propped on his hand as he studied blueprints. It wasn't until she got closer that she saw his eyes were shut.

He looked oddly boyish. There was something innocent and unguarded in his expression. She felt a weakening in her resistance to him.

"Jon." She put her hand on his shoulder, intending to shake him awake. Instead, it rested there like a caress.

His eyes snapped open.

"You were asleep."

"No, I was, uh, visualizing something on this design." He gestured to the blueprint in front of him then rubbed his eyes.

That gesture dealt a bigger blow to her resistance. She realized it wasn't only animal attraction pulling them together. She took a step backward as if to get away from the knowledge.

She cleared her throat. "I'm heading off now."

He gave her a smile, and she could see his exhaustion.

"Yeah, I should, too." He stood and stretched. The hem of his T-shirt rose as he arched his back and she caught a flash of hard male belly. She looked away, but it was too late. Her mind had committed the image to permanent memory.

And suddenly she knew, for good or bad, she'd never look at Jon the same way again.

Find out what happens next in ONE GOOD REASON, available August 2011 from Harlequin® Superromance®!

Copyright © 2011 Small Cow Productions Pty Ltd.

HSREXP0811

Celebrating **10** *years of*
Blaze™
red-hot reads

Featuring a special August author lineup of
six fan-favorite authors who have written
for Blaze™ from the beginning!

The Original Sexy Six:

Vicki Lewis Thompson
Tori Carrington
Kimberly Raye
Debbi Rawlins
Julie Leto
Jo Leigh

Pick up all six Blaze™
Special Collectors' Edition titles!

August 2011

Plus visit
HarlequinInsideRomance.com
and click on the Series Excitement Tab
for exclusive Blaze™ 10th Anniversary content!

www.Harlequin.com

HBCELEBRATE0811

Harlequin Presents®

USA TODAY *bestselling author*

Lynne Graham

introduces her new Epic Duet

THE VOLAKIS VOW

A marriage made of secrets…

Tally Spencer, an ordinary girl with no experience of
relationships… Sander Volakis, an impossibly rich and
handsome Greek entrepreneur. Sander is expecting to
love her and leave her, but for Tally this is love at first
sight. Little does he know that Tally is expecting his
baby…and blackmailing him to marry her!

PART ONE:
THE MARRIAGE BETRAYAL
Available August 2011

PART TWO:
BRIDE FOR REAL
Available September 2011

Available only from Harlequin Presents®.

www.Harlequin.com

HPI3005